Summer to Remember

Priscilla Maynard

SCHOLASTIC BOOK SERVICES
New York Toronto London Auckland Sydney Tokyo

Cover Photo by Owen Brown

ISBN 0-590-32166-8

12 11 10 9 8 7 6 5 4 3 2 1   4   2 3 4 5 6 7/8

~A~
Summer to
Remember

A Wishing Star Book

WISHING STAR TITLES
FROM SCHOLASTIC

ONE

CARRIE did not like him the minute she laid eyes on him. Arrogant was the word that came to mind. The way he held his head, it seemed as if he were looking down his nose . . . and then he singled her out. From behind lowered eyelids she watched him deliberately do so. Slowly, with confident ease, he turned toward her, then stood staring until their eyes met; then he smiled.

Twisting her head quickly, she looked away, but sitting there on the corral fence she felt a warm flush spread over her face, and she resented it, and him.

Yes, arrogant would describe him. She didn't even know his name, only that he and the other two men had come to work on the ranch during the spring and summer months. Her father had just picked them up from the Greyhound bus station in town. She knew nothing else about him.

It didn't matter. She would have no contact with him anyway. Besides, her parents preferred that she didn't mingle with the ranch help, except for Winger and Cleo, of course, who were permanent members of the ranch. They never had children and had now lived in the small wood frame house up on the hill for about twenty years. The other ranch hands came and went, so no one ever knew much about them.

Well, she thought, still averting her gaze, *that was just fine*. She needn't be bothered with him. Winger would see to that. And her father. It was just, well . . . she hadn't expected her father to hire someone so young. He couldn't be more than eighteen, but then, that could be deceiving.

She glanced back quickly. She watched him against her will as he walked away from the jeep with the other men and up toward the sleeping quarters on the opposite side of the barn, next to Winger's house. Winger was in the lead, not saying a word; walking with his same slow, long-legged swing. He was an extremely quiet man, not easily angered, but when he was, he spoke loudly and sharply, and with pointed words that one listened to carefully. It was Cleo who talked a blue streak in that family.

Her father had disappeared into the barn, and the jeep stood empty by the corral. She felt let down sitting there alone.

Carrie watched the three walk off. Little clouds of dust sprang up behind them as their cowboy heels dug into the powdery driveway.

One brown suitcase was all the young ranch hand carried. A cowboy hat hung low on his head, but black hair could be seen fringing his neck. Faded blue jeans hugged his hips, topped with a western-cut blue cotton shirt. He was neat, just dusty from the jeep ride. Measuring him against Winger, she guessed he was about as tall as her father, five ten or eleven perhaps; with a fairly dark complexion. His eyes were brown. She had noticed that, like her father's and brother's. Brown and large, in a rectangular face with high cheekbones. He wasn't handsome, yet he had an interesting face. One you would look at and ponder. Yes, arrogant with an interesting face. That might sum it up.

Carrie's eyes were deep blue like her mother's, her hair red and thick. It hung straight and long down her back, and framed her heart-shaped face, which held a small, slightly turned-up nose and large, dark-lashed eyes. A few freckles sprinkled her nose.

She sighed, then looked outward over the countryside, staring, not really seeing it as her thoughts drifted.

Yet, the countryside was worth gazing at. Colorado. The Courtley Ranch house and buildings sat cradled in the gentle, uprising slopes of the hills that graced a portion of the ranch lands. Flecked with pines, scrub oak, and outcroppings of huge, gray, weathered boulders, the hills rose gently, then sharply skyward, creating a constantly varied backdrop for the buildings nestled at the bottom. The house greeted the sun in the morning but never witnessed the setting sun because of the hills. The house was the typical two-storied country 1900-style house, and was freshly painted deep gray with white trim. The barn, which was really more of a large shed, stood weathered and bare to the north of the house and corral. Another shed, used as a garage, claimed a spot between the house and corral. Tall, conical shaped cedars, which her grandfather had planted as a wind break, stood soldier-like, close and touching, fencing the house to the west and to the north.

Acres of grazing land and fields planted each year spread eastward, northward, and to the south, almost encircling the hills. To the west the fairly level lands were stopped by a range of hills, rugged and wild. The whole ranch encompassed several thousand acres. It was a challenging enterprise.

Four generations of Courtleys had lived and worked the lands, and Mr. Allen Courtley had hoped his son, a fifth-generation Courtley, would continue the heritage of the land and the fierce pride of the family-held enterprise.

This wasn't to happen. Allen Courtley V had come to a sudden and untimely death after being thrown from a wild mustang he had captured in the hills. The horse was jet black and powerful, a magnificent creature. How thrilled Allen had been at the capture. It was a feat not easily attained single-handedly and one that took weeks of planning, often ending in disappointment. The conditions had been set by his father: He was allowed to capture the horse if done so fairly, with no modern conveyances . . . it was man against horse. Persistence was the key. He had his heart set on the wild beauty. Yet, in the end, the horse had won a terrible victory.

The mare was only fighting to be free, unaware of the grief and loss she left behind because of her fierce desire to regain her heritage . . . the freedom of the hills — a heritage inbred and instinctive in the mustang and one that spun back through time. The hills held the mustangs first. Who could blame the horse? No one. The animal returned to the rugged hills, her freedom won. She fled among the pines, up and out of sight, to join the herd of mares.

It was over. An emptiness hung deep and silent in the Courtley house. Young Allen was greatly missed. He had been a person of uncommon promise. Bright. Energetic. A bit too daring at times; he had a zeal untempered by wisdom. Some people said he was wild because of some of the feats he had attempted, but Allen was never malicious, never prone to harm another, and it was his own wild daring that brought him to his untimely end.

They all grieved. Grief. It has to be put in the back of the mind, shut out. Yet at moments least expected, it escapes, sometimes not even recognizable as grief at all, but some other unexplained emotion. It happens. Still, their daily lives continued. The sun rose, the rain and snow fell in their proper season like always, but Allen Courtley V was gone.

Four years had passed since his death. Carrie was now sixteen, the same age as when Allen had been killed. She, too, loved horses. The affection and sense of oneness between horse and rider was there for Carrie. Was it because of her brother or would it have flared naturally? Morning Star, her white mare, was Carrie's joy. The desire, however, to capture and train a wild horse held no intrigue for her. In fact, she stayed away from the hills. It was only a dark reminder, a sudden hollowness to catch sight of a fleeting mustang. Morning Star alone captured her attention and she looked no farther.

Carrie jumped from the corral fence and sauntered toward the house. Bonnie Lass, their black-and-white collie, came prancing from the shade of the few cottonwoods that grew between the garage and corral. With a quick backward glance, she saw Winger take the two into the adobe house that served as the sleeping quarters for the summer help.

"Let 'em work the wheat fields," she told Bonnie Lass, who acknowledged with a few wags of her tail. "Or the cattle or whatever. I'll be too busy with Morning Star to care about his smarty looks. Who does he think he is, staring like that?"

Bonnie Lass waved her plumy tail again. It was true. Her summer was full. She had to work and train Morning Star for the fairs and horse shows that she had entered months before the summer had arrived. The horse was ready to win ribbons. She knew it. At least she hoped her deep-felt assurance was right, and not just a pipe dream. No, she was sure.

Carrie ran her arm across her forehead as she walked. It was hot. Too hot for the end of April. She instinctively searched the sky, as any experienced rancher or farmer, whose dependence on weather is a vital link to survival. There was no inkling or promise of rain; only small puffy clouds scattered near the horizon.

Drought. The signs were apparent. Last winter's snow had been light, making the water supply meager. Now the spring rain rarely fell, and if at all, it was light, wetting only the surface soil, not affecting the low water table in the least. A bleak forecast for those who depended on the yield of the land.

Tomorrow her father would have the men finish sowing wheat. He and Winger had already begun the process weeks before and this would free them for other work on the ranch. Her father, she knew, was weather-worried. The crops. The cattle. He grew extremely quiet, keeping the trouble inside, his face rigidly set. His dark brown eyes, usually sparked with merriment, were now very serious. What good would talk do? Through the years the weather shifted, changed, threatened, raged, or blessed. Talk had nothing to do with it.

And now, for her and her mother, only two weeks of school were left. That was a relief.

She sniffed. "So that's why you're following me," she chided Bonnie Lass. "That's roast I smell." Why roast? Her mother didn't usually fuss much on a school night.

She walked up the cement stairs and across the wooden side porch. The wooden steps had long ago been replaced when they had rotted. The house was old. It had replaced the original log cabin three generations back. With each new generation, changes and improvements were made, but the basic turn-of-the-century design overshadowed any modern additions. It was still an old ranch house, comfortable and homey.

Clumping her boots extra hard so her mother would hear, she reached the screen door. Bonnie Lass, knowing the kitchen was off-limits during the supper hour, flopped on her old matted rug spread on the porch. Carrie knew she should have been in long ago to help. Instead, she had been perched on the corral fence being gawked at by a ranch hand. But a roast? How was she to know her mother would fuss about supper?

She opened the screen door. Her father always meant to oil it; anyone could do it, but perhaps the welcoming creek was a comfort. It sang . . . *I'm home.*

"I'm here," she called, entering the now modern kitchen, painted a soft pale yellow. Then she noticed the table pulled to its full extension and set for more than the family. "Who's coming tonight?"

Her mother stood at the kitchen sink washing lettuce and without looking up, answered, "The ranch help."

Carrie felt a sweep of resentment but with added zest at this intrusion. She'd have to sit through a whole meal with him? He'd probably stare the whole time. No doubt!

"Are you going to change clothes?" her mother continued.

Change clothes!

"No!" Carrie retorted.

"I only asked," her mother responded. She

glanced sideways at her daughter still standing near the door.

Change clothes! Jeans and a T-shirt are good enough. I'm not even going to comb my hair, she inwardly argued. *I may not even eat supper.* She began to plan how she might escape and work with Morning Star. The perfect excuse.

"Here, finish this," her mother said.

Without a word, Carrie washed her hands and began carefully dicing onions and tomatoes for the salad. The sun was below the hills now, leaving the kitchen dark. Carrie snapped on the light over the sink. "Why the fuss?" she asked. "Why can't they eat what we usually eat?"

Above the buzz of the electric beater, her mother asked loudly, "What?"

"Why the fuss?" Carrie said louder also.

Stopping the beater to stir butter into the mashed potatoes, she calmly got her answer. "The ranch help. They arrived late and it's right they get a good meal. Cleo will cook for them from now on, but she wasn't up to it tonight. We can guest them this one night."

Her mother always appeared calm. Not pretty, but attractive, the intense blue of her eyes illumined her whole face, making every other feature unimportant. Like Carrie, red hair crowned her head, and she wore it in different ways. Tonight it was braided and wound around her head.

Yes, always calm. Carrie sighed. Only when her brother had been thrown and killed had Carrie ever seen her mother crumble. For a long time after the accident, she had often heard her cry at night, sometimes walking about the dark house or sitting alone in the front room staring out the large window. It was quiet weeping. Alone weeping. Carrie had sometimes gotten out of bed to look, but she never intruded. As the grief subsided outwardly, the calm returned. It was necessary. Her mother taught English in high school, the same one Carrie attended. The students grieved, too, for they had lost a friend and fellow classmate. The tragedy struck them all, and an understood tenderness grew and remained between the students and teacher, her mother.

"What's wrong with Cleo?" Carrie demanded crossly.

Her mother looked up sharply. "What has set you off, Caroline Courtley?"

"Nothing," Carrie lied. "It just seems a bother when you have to teach tomorrow. I'm not hungry anyway. I think I'll give Morning Star a workout and skip supper. She needs it."

Her mother didn't answer. She spooned the mashed potatoes into a large bowl. Just then the jeep pulled up. Her mother handed her the bowl of potatoes to set on the table. Carrie felt panicky and trapped. The clumpy boots crossed the porch. The screen door creaked. Then, there she stood, face-to-face with him, still holding the bowl of mashed potatoes. Their eyes met. She was wrong. They were not brown but hazel, fringed with heavy black lashes. His face was unsmiling; only his eyes warm.

Carrie's eyes sought the floor. Then as hard as she tried not to, she blushed, her face flaming hot, her hands clammy. Why? She was with boys as much as with girls . . . maybe more. This had never happened. There was something that gnawed at her and brought up feelings that she did not understand or want. Yes, she definitely disliked him.

TWO

HURRIEDLY Carrie set the bowl on the table. Why, oh why hadn't she left before they had arrived! Hurrying back to the sink, she began to slowly stuff bits of lettuce and tomato down the garbage disposal and left Marc to stare after her. She had not even smiled. Nothing! He must think she's an idiot! Her father introduced the two to her mother. "Sarah, this is Charlie Colgate, and this here is Marc Bear. Charlie hails from around the Lubbock area, and Marc is from the south of Colorado, near the Oklahoma state line. He's going to the University of Colorado this fall."

Carrie snapped on the disposal switch, so that whatever this Marc Bear said in return she couldn't hear above the grinding noise. The kitchen window stood open, letting the downhill drafts of spring wind slip in and play with the curtains. How good it felt on her face! The wind not only sung of spring, but the promise of the coming summer. She could hardly wait. She stared out at the hillside, dreaming. Trees huddled on the steep slopes — shadowy but still visible while the sun's rays shot up like a crown from behind the summit.

Through the noise and into the dream came her mother's voice, louder than usual, "Carrie! Turn that off!"

She did so, feeling like a small child.

"We are ready," her mother continued more softly.

Marc and Charlie were coming back from washing their hands. True to her determined vow, Carrie had not changed clothes, nor combed her hair. Marc, however, had changed his dusty clothes and wore what appeared to be a brand-new shirt. The creases from the store fold were still apparent. Now that he wore no hat, his dark hair shone in the brightness of the overhead kitchen light. Charlie had not changed, but his slightly wavy hair had been combed with either water or hair goo and was slicked down, straight back. His blue eyes lit up easily, accompanied with an equally ready smile. It was a contrast to the solemn face of Marc Bear. He stood quietly near the doorway that led into the laundry room, watching.

The large oval oak table was at the far end of the spacious kitchen. Although it was part of the room, it had been made to appear separate by the use of hanging plants and a rug. A large picture window had been added by one of the generations of Courtleys, allowing the diners to gaze out at the flowerbeds with the tall cedars as a backdrop. The table was set with the in-between good dishes, not everyday, but not the best. A soft yellow tablecloth blended with the yellow of the kitchen and offset the green floral pattern of the china.

Carrie took her usual place at the table, to the left of her father. Marc watched, hesitated, then sought out the chair next to hers. She bristled, but at least she figured he couldn't stare at her. Then in an unexpected gesture, he pulled out her chair before she had an opportunity to seat herself. This threw her completely off guard. No one she knew did that, not for her anyway. Any boy she knew, well, it was more of a brother relationship: easy, comfortable, fun.

"Thank you," she mumbled. Thoughts swirled in her head and she made no attempt to stop them. No doubt he wants to impress my father and mom. What highfalutin' family did he come from? When grace was offered by her father, her inward grumbles were far from being of a prayerful nature.

"We eat big here, Marc," her father announced after grace, "so heap it high on your plate."

The bowls and platters were passed, quickly, silently, with all concentrating on the business of filling plates. Once the commotion of food passing was over, Mr. Courtley spoke, looking at Marc. "University of Colorado for you, eh? Good place for education and I'd recommend it for other advantages. It's where I met Mrs. Courtley. Right, Sarah!"

Mrs. Courtley nodded and smiled toward her husband at the opposite end of the table.

"I happen to be the first Courtley to ranch

using university know-how," he added. "And it helps . . . in all areas but one. The weather. No amount of degrees corners that!"

Marc acknowledged the remarks with a smile, then began to eat. The conversation circled among the adults, but he paid little attention, keeping his eyes mostly on his food. He was aware of Carrie, yet she didn't attempt any conversation, either.

Carrie, however, picked at her food, painfully aware that some kind of communication should be flowing between her and Marc. She should be treating him as guest and initiating the talk, however dumb or small. The tenseness grew with the prolonged silence; at least it seemed that way to Carrie. She was uncomfortable, but Marc just kept eating, and Charlie and her parents kept talking. Oh, she would rather be anywhere than here!

Her mother began to glance at Carrie, trying to catch her eye and frowning slightly in wonderment. Carrie gave her a weak smile and her mother returned it with a what-is-the-matter look.

"More roast, Marc?" Mrs. Courtley asked, hoping to ease the situation.

Without answering, he stabbed another large slice, smiled politely, and continued eating. It seemed the easiest thing to do. He must have decided that Carrie was very shy. After a few minutes, he stopped abruptly and half-turned toward Carrie. Yes, she was uncomfortable. He could see that, for there she was, pushing a piece of meat about her plate, her head down. His verdict had been right. The thick red hair hung over her shoulders, and with her head down, it fell forward, hiding her face from the side.

Hoping to make her feel more at ease, he spoke carefully. "My name is Marc Bear. You were busy at the sink when your father introduced us."

Without looking up or at him, Carrie muttered, "Hi," and continued picking and pushing the piece of meat about the plate. Then she put a few cooked carrots in her mouth and chewed much too long. Drat! He was still watching her. She could feel it, although she could not see his face.

"What year of high school are you in? Do you like school?" Marc asked.

"Yes," Carrie answered, ignoring the first part of the question. What a dumb question! Do I like school, she mimicked in her thoughts.

"Hear your mother teaches at the same high school," he went on.

"Yes," Carrie answered again. Why is he asking such questions if he already knows the answer? She poked a few more carrots. Maybe he'd stop asking questions if she ate. No such luck.

"Looking forward to the summer, I bet," Marc tried once more.

Sure," she said briefly, changing the response slightly. She felt utterly stupid. Yes! Yes! Sure! Yes, I was looking forward to summer! That is, until now! Why didn't he just eat?

That is what Marc had already decided to do.

She sure was a shy one. He bent his dark head over his plate and ate until it was empty. The others talked and laughed. Charlie was talking about the ranch he planned to purchase within the next year, and Mr. Courtley gave him his full attention as did Sarah Courtley.

A soft breeze tinged with a night chill wafted through the screen door while the glow of the final rays of sun completely faded beyond the hills. It was peaceful.

Marc peered about the room. It was homey, like his own home. A lived-in house. Neat, but not so painfully neat one would be uncomfortable. Shifting in his chair, having now finished his meal, Marc half-faced Carrie again. He'd try once more. Her long hair still hung like a curtain between them, but Marc was a friendly, outgoing person.

"Your dad told me you train and ride horses for shows. We talked a bit on the way from the bus station," he ventured.

"Yes," Carrie answered, stiffening. The answer was pointed, too curt.

Carrie, however, did not consider herself shy. A very private person, yes, and right now angry. Angry at her father. Why had he discussed her with a perfect stranger! Someone who came to work for a summer on the ranch. He did not need to know her business! Wait until later. She would tell her father just how she felt! Any thought of eating was gone.

Marc went blindly on: "I like to ride, too. In fact, I've competed at many fairs and horse shows. My grandfather gave me my first horse and also taught me more about horses than anyone." He spoke slowly, in a low tone so as not to interrupt the flow of the other table conversation.

Carrie's uneasiness touched Marc. If only he could make her feel comfortable enough to talk a bit, he was sure the timidity would fade. After all, having to take combat with three sisters all the time made him feel qualified to reach one shy girl. He bent his dark head just a little closer to the red hair that hid her face so well. "I understand your horse is called Morning Star . . . a mare. Mine is a mare, too. I'll miss training her this summer. I call mine Fleeting Cloud. She's white. It's interesting we both have chosen names from the sky. Fleeting Cloud is mostly mustang."

The conversation among the others had lulled momentarily, and the word *mustang* rang through the quiet kitchen like a bell.

Charlie Colgate, sitting across from Marc, was scraping his plate, not allowing one tiny morsel to escape. By the abundant shape of Charlie's stature and the manner in which he attacked the meal, it was plain that he had a passion for food. Scrape, scrape, scrape, Charlie went merrily on, but in spite of the continued scraping an intense silence filled the kitchen.

Mr. and Mrs. Courtley stopped chewing, glancing quickly at each other, then at Carrie. Even though Charlie helped himself to more potatoes, Marc felt the sting of the abrupt stillness instantly. It had to be something he said, since no one else had been talking.

He heard Carrie draw a sharp breath. Her hand held the fork, but she no longer toyed with the food on her plate. She sat as if turned to stone. The moment hung suspended.

What had he said? He spoke only of his horse, trying to draw Carrie out. What had he managed to do to offend this family his first night on the ranch? He certainly didn't want to make a negative impression, and that is exactly what he had done. He sat as still as Carrie.

Sarah Courtley began to slowly chew again, putting her fork on her plate. Her eyes shifted between Carrie and her husband. Mr. Courtley broke the brief silence by quickly turning to Charlie and beginning a discussion about the ranch. "Thought we'd finish sowing the wheat, hoping there will still be some rain this spring." Then he paused and glanced at Carrie, who had not moved.

Charlie nodded without too much of a break in his eating.

"More of anything?" Mrs. Courtley asked him.

Marc, still not knowing what he had said to bring the sharp break in the atmosphere, did not quite know what to do other than stare at Carrie, hoping for some sort of an answer. There was none.

With quick apprehension of Marc's dilemma, Mrs. Courtley leaned over, and quietly asked, "Marc, how about dessert? You look as if you're ready." She took his plate and in response, Marc turned from Carrie to her mother.

Marc felt a surge of relief. Mrs. Courtley rose, carrying her plate and Marc's to the sink, then he tuned in to what Mr. Courtley was telling Charlie about the work on the ranch.

At the word *mustang*, Carrie had drawn a breath as if stabbed, feeling the searing edge of the word. She had never known a mere word could cut like that. It hurt!

No, she was far from being over her brother's death. Far from it. Deep from the subconscious, the whole terrible scene of Allen being thrown from the wild mare burst forth. How many times had she relived that picture? How many times had it been a nightmare interrupting her sleep? How many times had she pushed it aside, leaving herself open for just such a moment as this?

And now that picture flashed. Brilliant. Real. There she was, standing next to the corral fence, watching who else but Allen. He was teasing, as usual. Showing off for her benefit. Sitting beside her was Bonnie Lass, whinning in a disturbing way. Standing, then sitting, but always whining. Allen sat on the opposite side of the corral, insisting he could ride the mare. He had the wild horse tied to a center post by a long rope, allowing her to reach the fence but not to go over it. "Look," he kept saying, "how calmly she walks the corral, not having bucked or kicked for days." She even ate from his hand. Proof of how far he had progressed in taming the wild creature.

Perhaps he had never meant to get on the horse. No one would ever know; but oh, how he loved to see his little sister react, which she did — and loudly. She always ran home to tattle. Her mother, not raised on a ranch, or with brothers, was secretly alarmed at her son's daring ventures, but she had learned to listen calmly to Carrie's constant tattling.

As he continued to insist he was going to ride, a real panic seized Carrie. This time she sensed the true danger. This was different from climbing the windmill as it whirled full speed, or seeing just how close he could get to a skunk, or riding steers when his father had forbidden it. The horse had no halter and was far from being ready for a bridle. There was just the rope. One around her neck, and to that was tied the center rope.

Allen had hollered, "I just want to see if she will let me put my leg over her back!" Bonnie Lass whined, nudging Carrie with her nose. Allen sat on the fence, urging the horse toward him with sweet things to eat. Probably sugar lumps. Softly, softly, softly, he spoke to the black horse. Ever closer she went to Allen until she stood beside him. Carefully he released the rope tied to the center pole, leaving only the rope around her neck! Again Bonnie Lass whined. At the same time, Carrie had yelled, "I'm going to tell Mother!" but instead of running, she stood glued to the spot, totally transfixed.

The horse ate what Allen offered, with only her eyes moving. That should have been warning enough. Bonnie Lass's tail sunk between her legs. *Run, run,* Carrie told her legs, but they did not move.

Slowly, ever so slowly, Allen had slid his leg over the back of the horse. Like a statue she stood, stiff, immobile. Then the mare's ears moved. They shifted from upright to flat. Allen hesitated. Even the dog was quiet now. It was like the earth waited in a vacuum, then it exploded. The black mare reared, throwing Allen to the ground, and in horror, Carrie watched as she trampled her brother until he no longer moved. Then that horse flew over the fence like Pegasus of the ancient myth.

Screaming, Carrie ran to the old school bell that hung near the cottonwood trees, between the garage and the corral. A bell that was rung only in warning or emergency. Carrie pulled with all her strength, screaming the entire time.

It all flashed, every detail, as if it were only yesterday instead of four years ago. So Marc rides a mustang! Oh, how glad she was that he could not see her face. She lowered her head still further. Tears of anger and hurt welled up, rimming her eyes, and any moment they might trickle downward. She fought them. Oh, why had her father hired this . . . this person?

The conversation moved slowly, not comfortably like before, but faltering. Her father continued talking to Charlie. Her mother came back from the sink to sit down.

"Excuse me," Carrie stammered. Abruptly she pushed back her chair, stood up, and, without looking at anyone, whirled about and shot out of the house.

Mrs. Courtley rose also, quickly, with a signaled glance to her husband, then she looked at Marc. He sat, bewildered, staring downward at the table.

"Carrie must not feel well," Mrs. Courtley excused her gently, smiling at Marc.

"That's too bad," Charlie said, sitting back. He sighed, patted his stomach. "Very good, Mrs. Courtley. Superior, I'd say. Superior." He sighed again.

"Thank you," Mrs. Courtley answered. She began to collect the rest of the plates and her husband rose to help her. "Then I assume you're ready for dessert, too. Marc, do you like cherry pie? Had it in the freezer all ready to bake. Actually, I made it during spring vacation a month or so back."

Marc gave her a quick nod and a smile, not quite sure of anything right now. He was still trying to figure out what had happened.

Outside, Carrie hurried toward the barn. Bonnie Lass trotted behind her. The tears she had fought so desperately in the house, now fell steadily, dripping from her chin, and she didn't bother to wipe them away.

"Why, Lassie girl, why?" Carrie asked the dog. The ache that had filled her days after the accident crushed any delight in the evening. The hush of the wind. Birds singing their closing hymns. The shadows, elongated, misshapen, still stretching on the prairie beyond the barrier of the hill, was all lost to Carrie. She ran past the corral and into the barn. The sweet scent of hay rose to meet her.

There was Morning Star. She needed to be pastured, but right now Carrie buried her face in her mane. "Why," she choked, "does that Marc make me feel like this?"

She bridled Morning Star, then climbed onto her back and without fussing with a saddle, rode out into the lingering twilight, wanting only to be alone.

THREE

THE last three weeks of school sped like the vanishing snow on the lower mountain slopes. Warmer days, clear and devoid of rain, kept confirming the prospects of a long dry summer. Carrie, busy with her exams and friends, thought little of Marc, seeing him only occasionally from a distance. He and Charlie now ate each morning and evening with Cleo and Winger, but each time Carrie happened to see Marc, she felt a fleeting desire to call out to her brother. To see Marc ride on the horses ridden by her brother was almost cause to call Allen's name and expect him to answer, only to be reminded each time that he wasn't there. She hadn't realized just how much she had missed her brother, or how empty the ranch had been these past four years. But the reminder came again and again: this was not Allen, no, not Allen, but a perfect stranger. She was determined to keep her distance from this constant jog at memories.

The last day of school came with flurry and fuss. There was the signing of the yearbook and good-byes, and promises to call or to write during the summer months. The last day, which lasted only until noon, sent Carrie home eagerly anticipating the summer. Her father had let her drive the pickup into town since her mother had to stay for the rest of the day, plus another full week, to finish up her records. What a relief not to have to drive back and forth for three wonderful months! As she sped out of town, her mind was filled with plans, but mostly, of course, for Morning Star. This was her summer! To train, train, train, and most importantly, to win. She had discussed it thoroughly with Debbie, her best friend. They would both train with Barney at Debbie's place. Oh, she couldn't wait! Never had she felt so full of expectation. She hummed and sang with the music that floated over the truck radio.

That evening she sat in her room checking and rechecking the calendar dates of all the competitions. There were seven in all, spread out fairly evenly through the summer, except for the two in August, which were only four days apart. Perched on one of the twin beds, Carrie, already in her robe, listened to some of her favorite tapes while she went over the dates. A hair clip held her long hair on top of her head.

From the front room she heard the phone ring and then her mother calling, "Carrie! It's Debbie!"

Jumping off the bed, she raced to the phone in the upstairs hallway. "Hi, Debbie!" she sang.

They talked for some time, laughing, giggling; then the conversation became serious. Carrie protested, then together, gloomily, they tried to figure out what they would do. After a while, Carrie promised to discuss it with her parents, then with a weak good-bye coupled with a frown, she hung up.

"Darn!" she muttered. Sitting on the floor next to the phone, she felt as if a cold bucket of water had just been dumped on her. "Darn!"

Slowly she got up and walked downstairs into the front room. It was almost dark in the spacious room — only one lamp burned. The soft glow heightened the gold of the rug within the circle of light, then tapered off in ever-darkening tones as the light receded to the dark corners of the room. Her mother sat on the sofa with a book, in the center of the light's glow.

One glance at her daughter's face made her put her book down. "What's the matter?"

Carrie plopped on the floor in front of the sofa. "Well, wouldn't you know! I can't believe it!" she complained.

"Believe what?" her mother questioned, concern showing in her voice.

"I can't believe now that school is out and I am all fired up to start training Morning Star, Barney is going to be gone for the summer. I just can't believe it," Carrie repeated in utter dismay.

"Barney? Where is he going? What will Debbie do with her horse now?" Her mother wanted to know.

"And Debbie and I had this all planned. The whole summer! Barney won't be back until some time in August. That's too late. It's too late!"

Carrie grumbled on, leaning back on the easy chair behind her and letting her head fall against the arm.

Her mother, still not having her question answered, asked once more. "Where is Barney going?"

And Carrie, still figuring out her own problem, asked, "Do you suppose Winger could help me? He knows the styles and gaits. After all, he did train Allen."

Her mother leaned forward. "Carrie! Barney? Is something wrong in his family?" she insisted.

"Oh, not really serious. He has to settle an estate back east and do some other things, and it will take a while . . . and can't wait. And I can't wait!" Carrie finally explained. "His mother died this last spring."

Sinking back, her mother sighed, "Well, I feel better now."

"Well, I don't!" Carrie fussed. "What about Winger . . .?"

"You'll have to ask your dad. No back-door politics, and don't assume anything. He may not want to go through that again," her mother counseled. "Your dad is in his office." She nodded her head in the direction of the small office that was off the front room.

"Did I hear a call for help?" Mr. Courtley shouted from the office. He appeared in the doorway, snapped off the light, and walked slowly into the front room. He looked worried. The lack of rain was beginning to affect the budget, and he had just been working on the ledgers.

Carrie rose, put her arms about him, and gave him a big squeeze. He squeezed back. "Now I know." He laughed. "You want something."

He sat next to his wife. Mr. Courtley was not an outwardly affectionate man, but he always enjoyed the closeness he had with his daughter; he usually gave her what she wanted if the request was reasonable.

Standing in front of her parents Carrie argued, "It's Winger that I need. I'm desperate! Barney is gone and I'm left to train that horse alone. Well, I can't do it alone!" She stopped, put her hands on her hips, and heaved a heavy sigh. "I can't! I'll have to cancel all the competitions. I've got to be good. Really good . . . like Allen would have been. Everyone expects it, and I think we can do it. In fact, I know it. But now, everything is falling apart!"

Her parents watched, listened, then stared as Carrie sank to the floor in front of them in despair. They said nothing.

"You don't think it's serious," Carrie said, frowning.

"Hold it, Carrie," her father cautioned. "Of course, we think it's serious. Are you through? Are you making a decision not to show, or are you asking for Winger's help?"

"Yes, I want Winger to help me, but if he can't, then I have to cancel," she explained. Her eyes widened, disappointment clearly reflected.

"Winger can help you, if that's what you need. The planting is done and anything else can be handled by Charlie and Marc for a while." Mr. Courtley answered.

Mrs. Courtley sat with furrowed brow. She pondered what Carrie had just said, about being really good. That was fine, but . . . like Allen? She didn't want to throw a damper on her daughter's spirits at this point, so she tucked it in a corner of her mind.

"Be sure that you consult Winger. He may not want to spend time training a horse. He's busy," her father emphasized.

The light returned to Carrie's eyes. "I promise," Carrie replied, her world once more coming into focus. "Thanks, Dad!" She turned and flew back up the stairs. She grabbed her calendar and marked, "Debbie — her house, on the June 23rd square."

Nine-thirty. It wasn't that late, but Carrie felt almost ready to sleep. It had been a full day. Walking to the window she gazed out into the night. She could see Morning Star out in the pasture, her white coat silvery in the full moon. Her eyes traveled from the pasture across the wide driveway to the corral. She shivered, although there was no reason to. It wasn't the breeze that fluttered the curtain. It was warm, although by morning it would be mountain-chilled. Bumpy little clouds hedged the moon as if trying to corral it.

She thought of Debbie. This may well be their last summer together with horse shows and such. Being a year older and a senior this coming year, Debbie would go away to college before Carrie did, leaving an empty place in her life. Few close friends had found their way into her world, and the ones she had, two, in fact, were her main contacts. Louise, or Lucy as everyone called her, had gone to California for two months, so this summer with Debbie would mean a lot. Slumber parties and other group-oriented gatherings had never appealed to Carrie, and the need for them was never felt. A ranch childhood of long days alone encouraged the art of imaginative play, for in this world, one is never really alone or bored. Ranch animals, especially Bonnie Lass, plus ponds teeming with frogs, fields where prairie dogs popped up like toast, soaring hawks, scurrying mice, all in the arena of haystacks, trees, heaps of gray boulders, and hills, tease the imagination into days filled with a special wonder. Along with her brother, this had been Carrie's world, rich and full of what others might find insufferably dull.

The bumpy clouds crowded out the moon, the moonlight filtering through creating a haze and accentuating the amount of clouds that had actually gathered in the sky. Carrie wondered. She hadn't listened to the weather report. Had rain been predicted? Leaving the window, she opened her bedroom door and called downstairs, "Did they predict rain tonight?"

Below, her father had just flicked on the television, waiting for the ten o'clock news. "Not that I know of," he called back. "Chances only, but then they've said that before and nothing happened."

But he was wrong, much to his delight. Rain fell for two days, off and on. A gentle rain that fell steady for hours, soaking the earth enough to coax the spring wheat to sprout. Carrie loved it, for the twinkle returned to her father's eyes and his whistle announced him before he appeared. Her mother, too, fussed in the flower garden when she came home from school in the rain.

Early in the second day of the rain, Carrie sought out Winger. She waited until Marc and Charlie had left for the day, watching from her bedroom window. When the jeep headed for the back range, she headed out of the house. Once beyond the barrier of the cedar trees, she ran, jumping the puddles all the way to the house on the hill. It was still raining, but she had not bothered with a raincoat or umbrella, and by the time she reached the back stairs and burst onto the screened porch, rivulets streamed down her face. Bonnie Lass had puddled-jumped with her and now sought the shelter of the porch, shaking vigorously amidst a self created shower. Normally, the dog was a welcomed member inside the house, but not today.

"Come in," Cleo called before Carrie had time to knock.

"Where's Winger? Is he here?" Carrie called back while still taking off her riding boots then went into the kitchen.

A wiry little woman, Cleo moved with deliberate speed. Right now she was cleaning the kitchen after cooking a hearty breakfast for the three men, but she stopped long enough to give Carrie a quick hug. Usually she wore jeans, but today it was slacks and a matching blue top, meaning she had something other than housework planned. Her short hair was curled as if she had just washed and set it.

"You look nice, Cleo," Carrie told her. "Going to town?"

"Yup. And you want Winger? Oh, I bet I know. . . . Morning Star. Your dad mentioned it," Cleo told her. "I think Winger plans on doing paper work today because of the rain. Not that he's complaining . . . he ain't. He's in the front room."

Carrie started in that direction.

"Say," Cleo continued, "that young ranch hand is really a nice boy."

Carrie's stomach tightened a bit along with her lips but not noticing, Cleo clucked on. "Really nice. So polite. And did you know that he's part Comanche? Grandfather, I think. You didn't know that, did you?" She looked so pleased; she loved getting news first.

Cleo was not a gossip. But she did talk, and, as she gathered people to her she surrounded them with her warmth and lots of talk. She had a way of connecting with people, her light blue eyes seeking others until the friendliness was established and confirmed.

"No, I didn't know, and I don't care to know," Carrie retorted much too curtly.

A bit of hurt flickered in Cleo's eyes. "Oh, honey . . ," she began.

Carrie realized too late how she had sounded. "Cleo, I'm sorry," she backtracked. "It's just, well, I'm not really interested in the ranch hands. You know."

Standing there next to the table, Carrie

33

looked at Cleo, trying to appear casual, not interested, although her tone had indicated something else. In return, Cleo intently studied Carrie. This girl, whom she loved as a daughter, did not fool Cleo for a second.

"Well, one thing I know," Cleo confirmed, "is that for some reason you are very unfriendly to this young man. I think it's deliberate, and it has nothing to do with not mingling or not being interested in the ranch hands. We've had young men before this. I've never seen you act unfriendly."

"Honest, Cleo, that isn't true," Carrie countered. "I'm just too busy, and Morning Star is more important. There is so much to do, and I need Winger's help."

Cleo wagged her head, not a bit convinced. "He's in the front room like I said, working on his papers."

"Thanks, Cleo. I knew you would understand," Carrie said, and scooted into the front room before anything more was said. She'd never fool Cleo, but she simply didn't want to talk about Marc Bear. Actually, she didn't know how to explain how she felt. How could she say he was arrogant? They wouldn't agree, so why discuss it?

The frame house was not very big, with the kitchen and front room dividing the first floor, the front room taking two-thirds of the floor space. Upstairs there nestled three bedrooms under the eaves, along with a small bathroom. This was the house to which Winger had brought Cleo as a bride some twenty years ago, and it was the only home they had ever known. They never had children, but both the Courtley children thought of Cleo and Winger as second parents.

While Cleo was talkative with an easy, ready laugh, Winger was quiet. Winger—tall, six feet and some in his stockings—was again a contrast to his tiny five-foot wife, yet Cleo took over like a general where Winger was concerned. How she fussed over him! Winger said nothing as she talked and fussed, silently relishing the devotion. He could tease, too, however, as Carrie well knew. But he shared his quiet warmth easily and readily with his family. Many times Carrie had cuddled in his lap while he had read or told her stories.

As she entered, he looked up from his desk in the corner, expecting her. "Well, Kitten, what can I do for you? Your dad said you had a favor to ask, so ask; but remember, I might just say no," he cautioned, his face a mask of seriousness, only his eyes giving him away.

"Do you have time," Carrie asked hurriedly, in case he might be serious, "to help me with Morning Star? It's her changing gaits that really need work. I think we're ready to win. I've got to place high. I've got to do it, Winger!" Her voice was hedged with tension that spoke of her determination.

Uncrossing his long legs, Winger stretched them out in front of him. With his pointed western boots, his large feet looked even larger. He crossed his arms, tilted his head back, and peered at Carrie. Carrie wiggled her toes in the rug, waiting.

"Winning, eh? Now, why is winning so all-fired important?" Winger asked.

"What are you talking about? Do you think I want to compete *not* to win?" Carrie asked in return, wrinkling her face into a frown.

Winger still peered down his nose. "Now, now, settle down. What I'm getting at is this. Are you working for your best, or simply to win? Working just to win will make you nervous, up-tight, and might even make you lose your perspective. What is it you want me to help you do?"

Carrie didn't answer. The frown remained.

Then, very softly, Winger added, "Are you competing with yourself, or" — and he paused — "with your brother?"

Silence. Her lips clamped tighter. It made her angry to hear him say that. So what if she wanted to ride as well as Allen? What difference did it make to anyone? Wasn't it right to uphold her brother's image through her own riding; and the Courtley name?

Winger saw the result of his well-intentioned lecture and retreated. He sighed. "Of course, I'll help you. Say, I just had an idea. That Marc Bear is terrific with a horse, maybe . . ."

"No!" Carrie exploded.

Winger jerked his head up, his eyes widening. "Okay! Okay!" He retreated again. "Don't snap my head off. What have you got against Marc Bear?"

From the kitchen Cleo called, "I told her what a fine boy he is!"

That did it! Carried headed for the kitchen and the back porch. She turned long enough to ask very quietly. "When can we start?" She didn't want to rile Winger. He could get very angry. It took some doing, but he could and then, he might not help her.

"Why, tomorrow, if the rain stops," Winger answered, looking baffled.

Carrie nodded, turned, and fled.

FOUR

THE rain did stop, and she and Winger began in earnest to bring Morning Star to top performance. Winger was working for best performance while Carrie was working for a winning performance.

The entire morning was spent in a rigorous workout. While training, Winger changed completely, dropping the warm family relationship, emerging as an unrelentless dictator. Again and again he made Carrie go through the paces. He barked commands like an army sergeant. Sit straighter! Head up! Hold the reins looser, then tighter. They would take a short break, then back to work. Morning Star looked good. Her beautiful white coat glistened in the sun. She had the makings of a top show horse. It was all there.

But to Carrie's annoyance, Marc kept going in and out of the barn, driving the jeep close to the fence, stopping to watch for short periods of time. After the third time, Carrie flared like a testy mother cat. When he sped off with his usual calm assurance, Carrie jumped off Morning Star and approached Winger with anger written all over her. She shouted, "Why isn't he somewhere else? Why does he stare at me?"

Winger, with his easy manner, pushed his hat back slightly, puckering his lips as he gazed down at her, and finally demanded, "What's wrong with you, Carrie? He's only interested in horses, and showing horses. Besides, you shouldn't even be aware of him. You're the one at fault. If you were concentrating properly, a dragon wouldn't bother you."

"Well, he bothers me with his staring," she insisted.

"That's your problem, and you'd better get over it now because when you're in that ring you're going to be stared at plenty, Winger said firmly. "I told you he was an excellent horseman. You might do well to speak to him about horses."

"Fat chance!" Carrie exclaimed. "You taught Allen everything he knew and look how good he was! Why should I listen to a perfect stranger?"

Shaking his head, Winger could see this was leading nowhere. Carrie remained defiant about Marc Bear. Inwardly Winger smiled, but only inwardly. Gazing down at Carrie, he had an inkling about the situation. But there she stood, her mouth stretched in a tight line, her eyes wide with nothing but aggravation.

"Get back on your horse, Kitten," he directed. "We don't have time to waste."

Still ruffled, Carrie mounted and they finished their morning session. Marc didn't appear again, but a negative tone was there. When they were done, Winger became his old self again, and they went off in their own directions for the rest of the day.

The next morning Carrie went into Prairie View with her mother for a dental appointment, getting back to the ranch about eleven. As they drove into the garage, her mother wanted to know about lunch.

"I can't feel my mouth yet," Carrie told her.

"Soup, maybe," her mother said. "I'll cool it so you won't burn your mouth."

They gathered a few packages from the backseat and walked slowly toward the house. It was an exceptional day: warm, the air clear and refreshed after the rain. May was over. Monday, June 2nd, would be the first of her shows, and it was right in Prairie View. That pleased Carrie, for she would ride back and forth with her father. It was a time to be alone with him for three whole days. She smiled at the prospect, for that didn't happen very often.

After her brief lunch, she rushed to join Winger at the corral. Ooooops! He was just leaving his house. She should be all saddled and ready to go. Now he would fret. Winger did not like to waste time. She ran faster. Boy, she sure enjoyed him more when he was just Winger and not trainer.

"Ready?" he called when he saw her running toward the barn.

"One minute," she yelled, and she disappeared into the dark of the barn. She stopped short.

There was Morning Star, all saddled, ready to

go, waiting in her stall. She had put the horse in the barn that morning before going to the dentist, but who had saddled her? No one was in the barn. "Winger!" She laughed. "Who else?" Under his mask of toughness as a trainer, he was still Winger.

"Well, you are ready after all," he declared as she led the horse into the corral.

"Of course," Carrie quipped. "As you well know."

"And how would I know?" Winger asked. "Don't talk in riddles, Carrie. Let's get going."

As she swung into the saddle she questioned him. "Didn't you saddle Morning Star?"

"Nope!" was his short answer, and he started.

Then who? Instinctively Carrie knew who. Marc! He wasn't even in sight, and he made her upset. He just wasn't going to stay out of her way.

As the sun went down at about four o'clock, Marc drove from the northern range with Charlie. They skidded to a dusty stop in front of the barn, clambered out, and draped their tired selves on the corral fence to watch.

Carrie became immediately aware of them. She felt her stomach twist into knots. Darn it! Winger would know it right away and be all over her. From the corner of her eye, she saw the two of them talking, pointing, and nodding. She did more than tense up, she messed up — and good.

Winger jumped off the fence like a firecracker just lit. He shouted, pointing at her, "Concentrate! Concentrate! You can't let people break your concentration! Do that gait again! And do it right!"

Charlie left, but Marc remained by the fence, still watching every move. Carrie did the gait again, and then again, but it was over for the day. Winger knew it and so did Carrie. Even Morning Star strode toward the gate. With his long-legged stride, Winger walked over to Carrie at the gate. He patted her, smiled, and added gently, "Good workout, Carrie. There's improvement."

She watched him go through the gate and head for his house. It was then she saw her father. He was coming from the house, and walked quickly toward the corral. Carrie was ready to go and speak with him, but he went straight to Marc.

"Son?" he said.

Carrie jerked, stiffened. Was her father speaking . . . to Marc? Son! She felt as if she had been slapped, hard. How could he call Marc son?! Quickly, she went through the gate and edged Morning Star in their direction.

Her father repeated, "Son? Could I ask a favor of you?"

What now? Carrie thought.

"Carrie, here, has a horse show this Monday," and her father smiled up at her as he spoke. "I have other business that Winger and I can't put off. Do you suppose that you could drive her into Prairie View and back for three days? I would sure appreciate it."

Carrie was horrified. She couldn't believe her ears.

Marc straightened up. "Yes, sir," he volunteered. "I'd be happy to help you out."

The two smiled at each other, then Marc smiled up at Carrie. There was no smile in return, so he turned and hurried off toward the adobe bungalow.

Even before he was safely out of earshot, Carrie protested. "Dad, how could you?" She jumped off Morning Star.

Her father, startled, drew back. Puzzlement filled his eyes. "How could I what? Is there something wrong?"

"Wrong?!" she exploded. "I don't want him to take me! I want you or Winger!"

He relaxed and smiled. "I can't do it, Carrie. Marc isn't going to bite, you know. I wouldn't ask him if he weren't responsible. He is." A twinkle lit his eye as he looked at his daughter's pleading face. He pinched her cheek lightly. "You know, you're as pretty as your mother." Then he left, leaving Carrie standing there steaming mad.

FIVE

MONDAY morning dawned cloudless with the usual early chill, but by eight o'clock the sun was beginning to prove it was summer.

Carrie woke to a sun-filled room. The brightness matched her expectations and hopes for the day. She wasted no time daydreaming, but shot out of bed to shower and dress. Before making her bed, she paused at the window. There was only one shadow on the day. Marc. He had already hitched the horse trailer onto the pickup and was heading for the pasture to get Morning Star. Walking in that self-assured swing, he whistled some catchy tune.

"Well, I'm glad he's happy about this," Carrie mumbled to herself. How could he be so much like Allen? Even that cocky swagger. Of course, cowboy boots always made one swagger. But it was more than that. It was the way he was built and the agile manner with which he handled himself. Carrie sighed. She sure wished Allen could see her ride today, and she doubly wished her father were driving her into Prairie View.

She'd better get going. Marc would soon have Morning Star in the trailer, and she should be ready. She whipped through making the bed, which would pass no inspection, then raced downstairs into the kitchen.

Her mother had her place set, and she saw that her father had already eaten. Only his coffee cup was left at his place, which meant he was still around and would return.

"I'm not hungry, Mother," Carrie said.

"Hungry or not, some food is going into your stomach. What you don't need is to be queasy from the lack of food," her mother answered firmly.

Carrie went to the refrigerator to get some orange juice and poured a full glass. "This will be enough, with some toast," she said, going to the table to sit down.

"No," came the firm answer, and a plate of scrambled eggs with toast was set in front of Carrie.

Her mother examined her momentarily. Carrie's face was already flushed with excitement. The flush of her cheeks accentuated the brightness of her blue eyes. Her usually free-flowing hair hung in one long braid down her back. Mrs. Courtley had a surge of pride, which always accompanies the love one feels toward another. She told Carrie again, "Eat."

Bonnie Lass began to wiggle and fuss on the porch, making her dog-talk noises. Mr. Courtley was coming, and then the clump of his boots on the porch. As the squeaky screen door banged behind him, he greeted Carrie. "Well, Rapunzel, are you ready for your big day?"

"A humph was her answer.

"Still mad, eh?" he teased. "Now, I think many a girl would jump at the chance to ride with Marc Bear."

Carrie paused with a forkful of eggs halfway to her mouth, and the flush of her face heightened.

"Let it drop, Allen," Mrs. Courtley cautioned gently from the other side of the kitchen, her eyebrows raised.

He nodded, then helped himself to another cup of coffee from the electric pot on the table. "You will do well today. Winger says you've made good progress."

"As good as Allen?" she inserted quickly.

Her father put his cup down. "He didn't compare you to Allen. He just said your progress was good."

"I have to be as good as Allen, Daddy," Carrie said, her chin set.

There was no answer. She went back to eating her eggs while her father began to read some papers he had brought to the table with him. The only sound in the kitchen was the clinking of dishes and running water as her mother rinsed the breakfast dishes.

Carrie's new riding habit hung in a plastic bag beside the back door. It was navy blue, and the accompanying white shirt had frills down the front and at the cuffs, which would extend a bit beyond the sleeves. There were also new riding boots, not the western style, but traditional calf-hugging ones.

Two short horn blasts brought them up short.

"Marc is ready," Mr. Courtley announced, looking up from his newspaper to glance at his daughter.

"I know," she answered simply, but somehow she couldn't make herself get up from the chair. She was going to be trapped with him for an hour driving into town, and she had funny swirling feelings in her stomach. It was more than her first horse show, she knew. She was afraid to be alone with Marc. What in the world would they talk about for an hour? She didn't like him, but he was being so kind to her.

Her father rose from the table, leaving his papers next to his coffee cup. "Let me help you," he offered. "I'll take your things to the truck while you collect yourself."

"I'm not ready," Carrie fretted. "I've got to brush my teeth."

"Calm down, Carrie," her mother said. "He'll wait."

For ten minutes Carrie dashed about the house, thinking of any little thing to do, until it became obvious to her mother.

"Carrie! Marc is waiting!" she called up the stairs.

In the kitchen again, Carrie looked sheepishly at her mother.

"Are you that scared?" her mother asked.

They stood together at the door.

Carrie shook her head. "Not so much of riding, but . . ."

"It's Marc, isn't it?" Mrs. Courtley asked, gazing intently at Carrie.

"Why can't Daddy take me, or Winger . . . or even Charlie?" Carried pleaded.

"He can't. And, you know your father would take you if he really could. He feels badly enough about it. Don't you fuss," her mother said gently, but firmly.

"But I don't like Marc. I don't want to be with him," Carrie insisted.

"Why not?" her mother asked.

"I don't know. He bothers me and makes me feel upset," Carrie tried to explain.

Her mother looked directly into her eyes. "He reminds you of your brother, doesn't he?"

"I guess," Carrie answered.

"Well, you be kind to him. That's not his fault. Now, you get out there, or you'll have your father on your tail." And as she spoke she gave her daughter a hug. "You'll do well."

Winger and her father stood talking on the far side of the pickup, and Marc was already behind the wheel. He made her nervous just sitting there. Maybe her father or Winger would take her tomorrow, but her mother had warned her not to make a scene. She'd wait to see what tomorrow would bring. Hopefully, not Marc.

"Well, Carrie, I thought you might have gotten lost," her father said. "Come on, it's going to be a full day.

Reaching out, Winger grabbed Carrie and lifted her up to eye-level then, looking her squarely in the eyes he said, "Now Kitten, you do your best."

"Thanks, Winger. Put me down. I want to go

talk with Morning Star before we leave," and once on the ground, she scooted back to the trailer. Actually, she felt foolish being treated in this babyish manner in front of Marc. It was Winger's way. He had always shown his affection openly, but where Marc could see? She ran around to the trailer to hide her embarrassment.

Marc sat, drumming his fingers on the steering wheel, the only evidence of any impatience to be off.

Finally Mr. Courtley opened the passenger door and said, "Hop in, Carrie, or you'll be late."

She had stalled long enough. She slid in beside Marc, and her father slammed the door shut. Off they went with a wave from everyone.

They headed down the long driveway, going slowly to accommodate the horse trailer. Carrie decided she'd just watch the scenery and think about her riding. The plastic bag with her riding habit was between them, and she was glad. It was almost like another person sitting there, silent, but there.

Once they reached the county blacktop they could drive faster, and Marc drove at about fifty miles per hour, just at the limit. He drove with assurance. He does everything with assurance, Carrie thought. But at least it made her feel comfortable; so, she looked out of the window as she had decided to do. After a bit, she took out her sunglasses from a small handbag she carried.

There! That was better. There was something about sunglasses. They made you feel hidden. You could look out, but no one could look in.

Carrie took a sidelong look at Marc. He kept his eyes on the road, his face calm and without expression. Whatever he was thinking didn't show. The cowboy hat he always wore sat slightly back on his head, a bit different from the way he usually wore it, and his firm profile was more apparent. His nose was medium in size and straight, being slightly rounded on the end. He had high cheekbones, giving evidence of his heritage, and the chin was strong. He must have felt Carrie studying him, for he shifted, turning his head toward her.

Her eyes fled back to the scenery and there they stayed. She thought of switching on the radio but didn't. Halfway into Prairie View, Marc tried to make conversation, only to be met with silence, or a brief yes or no. Carrie had definitely made up her mind that Marc was not going to bother her or intrude in her life. In no way! Nothing Marc said broke through the wall that Carrie had started to build on the very first day they had met. Finally he gave up. Silence between them settled, heavy and uncomfortable. It was Marc who switched on the radio.

Again from behind her sunglasses, Carrie glanced sideways at Marc. His face was blank. She could read nothing. That was it. The remainder of the way there was only the music. Carrie was relieved when they reached the fairgrounds. Signs guided them to the horse barns, so Carrie didn't have to direct Marc, but once in the parking lot Marc spoke. "You go and take care of the necessary paper work," he said, "and

I'll take Morning Star out. Let me know her stall number."

"All right," was all she answered, not looking at him. His commanding tone of voice threw her, sending darts of guilt through her. She had not listened to her mother — she had been unkind, yet it appeared reasonable to her. How else could she contend with the feelings that arose every time she was near Marc? She wasn't acting this way just to be mean. She headed for the office, which was at the far end of the horse barn. Peering over her shoulder, she saw that Marc was already opening the gate of the trailer.

Nine o'clock. She'd better hurry. Entering the semigloom of the barn, Carrie removed her sunglasses. She had not entered directly through the office, which was tucked in one corner of the huge structure, so she walked half the length and the width of the barn. This half was empty, and as she walked the smell of clean hay surrounded her. There were bales stacked in the empty stalls.

The door of the office was open. One person manned the desk, a woman. There was no one else in the small office.

"Can I help you?" the woman asked, peering through a pair of huge-rimmed glasses.

"Yes. I'm Caroline Courtley. I've entered the horse show," Carrie told her while handing her an entry form.

The woman took the paper, scanned it, then turned to check a list by running her finger down a long line of names. "Courtley. Courtley," she kept repeating. "Ah, here we are. These are not in alphabetical order, but numerical, so you were near the end."

She gathered Carrie's riding numbers and handed them to her, and a stall number for Morning Star. Then she put a check mark next to Carrie's name. "Oh, yes, you'll need the time schedule so you know when to ride. By the way, are you Allen's sister?"

"Yes, I am," Carrie answered, feeling that pride that people would know and remember him.

"Well I thought so, since there is only one Courtley family in these parts. Hope you ride well, and if you ride half as well as your brother, you'll do fine," the woman said, and smiled.

"Thank you," Carrie returned. "See you." This time she used the door next to the office rather than walk back through the barn. The glare of the sun made her squint and the heat that radiated from the yellow, hard-packed earth hit her with force. Carrie grabbed for her sunglasses and pulled her western hat down farther to shade her eyes. Being able to open her eyes fully was a relief. "Whew!" she sighed.

It was then that she spotted Debbie, with John and Kathy walking slowly across the fairway, away from the barn. She saw Kathy and John only at shows like this. They were more friends of Debbie's, but she always enjoyed being with them.

"Debbie!" Carried shouted. "Debbie!"

The three of them turned.

"Wait up!" she hollered louder.

The day was becoming a real scorcher. As she started out to join her friends, the sun beat down as if it wanted to melt her to a puddle, and there was not a nip of a breeze to temper it.

"Hi, Carrie," Debbie said, accompanied by one of her ready smiles. "I tried to call last night, but your line was busy."

"It was probably Dad. He has a lot of business right now," Carrie explained. "Where are you headed?"

John spoke. "To the cafeteria. It's going to be a long day, and for me, breakfast was a long time ago."

"That's John! Stomach first!" Debbie laughed. "Come with us." She pulled Carrie's arm as she spoke.

"When do you ride?" Kathy wanted to know.

"Well, let's see," Carrie said, consulting the time schedule she had just received.

"Do we have to stand in the sun here in the midddle of nowhere?" John complained. "I see some nice shade right over there."

He referred to a long shadow cast by a building on the opposite side of the fairway. In silent agreement they all headed for it. Once in the shade, Carrie again consulted her timetable. The three of them waited, gazing intently at her, and she knew what was going on in their heads. "One o'clock," she finally figured.

"Are you scared?" Kathy asked, being very direct.

"Are you?" Carrie countered.

"Well, I don't have a brother who just happened to be the best rider in the area," Kathy reminded her.

John cut in, "Hey, that is heavy, Kathy. Leave her alone." Carrie shot him a grateful look. "Besides," he continued, "I'm starved. Are we going to eat or aren't we?"

Carrie was suddenly glad she had to go and give Marc the stall assignment. "I need to go back to the trailer. Marc is waiting for Morning Star's stall number."

"Marc! So that's your new ranch hand! Saw you drive in a while ago. Young, isn't he? Will you introduce us?" John asked teasingly.

"Later," was her answer.

"Where is he from? I heard that he rides well. I think Winger told my father. Don't be so mysterious . . . later, is all she says," John imitated.

"Well, then maybe Winger told your father where he was from, too," Carrie shot back.

"Touchy. Touchy. Say, is there something between you two and you want him all to yourself?" John asked, squinting his eyes as if looking through her like a detective.

Disgusted with the conversation, Carrie announced "I've got to go. If you want to meet him, John, go and introduce yourself."

Debbie said nothing, not wanting to add more spark to fire, but Kathy picked up the theme.

"Why all this touchiness about a ranch hand?" she asked. "Is he an enchanted prince, or something? Will he turn into a frog tonight when you go home?" She wrinkled her nose and laughed.

"He works for my father, that's all. Today he brought me because my father had other business," Carrie explained curtly. Usually their teasing didn't hit her like this, but then, they had never teased her about a boy. The teasing really made her burn. No way would she introduce them to Marc Bear. Not now. They were reading stupid meanings into everything. "See you later," she added, waved, and headed back across the gravely fairway to the trailer.

"Only teasing!" John hollered after her.

She waved but kept going.

The rest of the day was no better. In two showings, at one o'clock and two-thirty, she placed tenth and fifteenth. That was a far cry from winning or even placing near the top.

As she rode Morning Star out of the ring after the second show, it was obvious to everyone that she did not ride like her brother. It was even more obvious to her. Disappointment rested heavy on her shoulders. Winger had warned her and more indirectly, so had her parents. Aside from wanting to ride like Allen herself, she felt everyone there expected her to. She had felt it, like a cloud hanging over her head, and she had let it break her concentration. The disgust that welled up inside her was almost greater than the disappointment. But what stung most was the feeling of letting Allen down . . . not upholding the Courtley name.

Outside the arena, she dismounted, smiling at everyone, keeping her composure. She had to be a sportswoman above all, and there she would not fail. The usual little comments followed her. Good riding! Beautiful horse! All the polite things said. What they said when she wasn't there was another matter, no doubt. Well, let them talk!

The stall area was busy and she had to walk Morning Star clear to end of the aisle. Others were coming and going or caring for their horses, but they all stopped to say something to Carrie. Actually, she began to see that they felt as badly as she did. Marc was nowhere to be seen. She was glad for that. *Had he watched her ride?* she wondered. She hoped not. The walls of the stall made her feel freer to be herself. She didn't have to smile at Morning Star and pretend to be brave, because she didn't feel brave. Not one bit. Leaning her head against the warmth of Morning Star's neck, she let the bitterness mingle with a few tears. After taking the saddle off, she began giving Morning Star a good rubdown. Softly, she spoke to the horse, patting, rubbing, soothing. Somehow Morning Star knew Carrie was not herself. Tossing her white head she let Carrie understand things were not right.

"It's all right, girl," Carrie soothed again and again.

"How you doing?" came a question from the aisle.

It was Debbie.

"I'll make it," Carrie answered.

Debbie came farther into the stall. "You did your best, Carrie," she comforted. "You can't ask for more than that." She could see that her friend was on the verge of tears and some had already spilled over.

But Carrie had other opinions. She shook her head, admitting, "No, I didn't! Far from it!" She rubbed harder on Morning Star's back.

"Carrie, you did!" Debbie argued. "You're not Allen."

"So, I'm not Allen!" Carrie exclaimed, stopping the rubdown to face her friend. "But I am a Courtley and I could have done better!"

"Carrie, you know what people are going to do when they hear the name Courtley? Compare you to Allen. I heard them in the stands all the while you were riding. Not his style. Not his command, and so on. Even after four years they haven't forgotten just how good he was. After all, the same people come to this horse show year after year. It's not your fault." Debbie tried to make the truth of the matter clear, and yet not hurt her friend.

"It isn't fair . . ." But she stopped and went back to grooming Morning Star.

Kathy and John approached Carrie apprehensively. Before Carrie turned around and saw them, Debbie shook her head, cautioning them.

"Oh, hi," Carrie greeted them with a weak smile.

"Why isn't Marc helping you curry your horse?" Kathy asked, looking around.

Carrie knew she just wanted to meet him, so she snapped, "Because I want to do it myself, that's why!"

The three raised their eyebrows and changed the subject.

"What time will you be here tomorrow, Carrie?" John cautiously asked.

"Why?" she wanted to know.

"Well, I'm on at ten, and boy, I need all the moral support I can get," he said.

Touching John's arm, Carrie said, "I'll be here because I know how you feel. Believe me. Will you cheer me on at two?"

"It's a deal," he agreed, then smiled at Kathy and winked. Even Carrie smiled. "Well, we got one smile out of her."

"Okay, but I'd better be going. See you tomorrow!" Then Carrie left them standing in the stall and headed for the parking lot. She just wanted out. She needed to be alone, to think and soothe her wounded pride. The semigloom of the empty half of the barn was the route by which she chose to leave. On the opposite side, the huge door stood open; the brilliance of the day was framed against the dim of the barn's interior. It led directly to the parking lot. She had not even bothered to change out of her riding habit. Her jeans and western boots were held tightly in one hand, having grabbed them as she fled from the stall. Now, she hoped Marc was at the truck.

They had parked in the second lane, so she wound her way among the many trucks and horse trailers. So far, no Marc. She should have made arrangements to meet, but then she had no idea things would turn out this badly. Normally, she would have taken time to be with Debbie and the others.

But this time she couldn't wait to leave. She'd soon be home. Home! As she approached the pickup Marc glided over to the door and opened it for her. She slid in without a word. Their eyes met momentarily as he slammed the door shut. Before Marc was seated behind the wheel she had put her sunglasses on, leaned her head back and receded into a world of her own.

There was no music. The roar of the engine was a comfort, and the empty horse trailer rattled over the gravel parking lot until they reached blacktop. Carrie sensed that Marc looked at her a number of times, but with her eyes shut she couldn't be sure. As much as she wanted to ignore him, she was only too aware that Marc was sitting beside her. The very strength of his being and his confident movements as he drove the pickup filled the cab. It reminded her of Allen. It was Allen that she wished were sitting next to her so she could talk and confide. She felt the emptiness of the loss. She had felt it in the show ring and in the barn.

The silence continued. Carrie decided Marc had not watched her ride, therefore he had no comment. Either that or he was not going to chance another rebuff like the one he had received on the way to the fairgrounds. Carrie was secure in the silence, wrapped in the thread of her own thoughts.

Then Marc spoke. "I am really sorry, Carrie. I know you had your heart on placing higher."

Her eyes shot open! He had watched! Her hands clutched tighter at the jeans and boots she held in her lap. "It doesn't matter," she lied, willing to stop the conversation right there, but unfortunately he continued.

"I'll help you, if you want," he innocently suggested. "I saw where you made your mistakes." The offer held kindness.

With her eyes wide in disbelief, she turned to meet his gaze. His soft hazel eyes were filled with expectation.

Stiffening, Carrie smartly replied, "Winger will help me."

This time the rebuff registered in Marc's eyes and flickered across his face, but blank indifference masked his feelings instantly.

Gone was the quiet, relaxed atmosphere.

Inwardly Marc sighed. His knuckles whitened on the steering wheel. This girl was certainly a mystery . . . a cold mystery. He, too, wished her father had driven her into the fairgrounds. Well, now what? He didn't want to offend the daughter of the boss and jeopardize the summer job that he needed so desperately. Apologize. Yes, that is what he would do.

Slowly he started, not sure what to expect. "Well Carrie . . . I didn't mean to offend you. Forget that I offered, if you feel that I've interfered. It's just that I've had to work out some of the same problems with my horse, Fleeting Cloud. That's all."

Marc braced himself.

"I don't care about Fleeting Cloud *or* your

help. My brother would know exactly what to do, knowing more about it than you ever will!" The words shot out like aimed bullets.

"Your brother? Where is he?" Marc asked in complete surprise.

"It's none of your business!" Carrie stated flatly, then clamped her mouth shut, trying to maintain her composure. Tears started at her eyelids. She would not cry. Not in front of Marc. She shut her eyes and fought the tears.

Marc, stunned, said nothing, and that is how it remained for the rest of the drive home. Strained silence.

SIX

*T*HAT evening, Marc gratefully washed for supper, relieved the day was over. What a day! He thought about it as he washed. He only hoped he had not messed things up so that something would be said to him. Carrie evidently wanted to keep him in his place, as a ranch hand. Yet he wondered. No one else treated him like that. Winger? Mr. Courtley? No, not one of them.

The cool water felt so good running over his hands and on his face. Charlie had already washed and gone to Winger's house. Charlie! He sure liked to eat. Well, so did he, Marc decided, and he had better get over there if he wanted to be fed.

He and Charlie spent little time in the adobe bungalow. To sleep and clean up was about it. Sunday was the only day they lingered at all, but even then, they found something to do outside on the ranch. Usually, anyway. Charlie liked to make things out of wood for his children. That he did outside. Marc liked to record his impressions of the ranch, of people and experiences. He tried to spend an hour or two typing on a Sunday morning, but otherwise, he was outside.

During the week their day was long. There was little left to the evening and weariness made them seek their beds early.

Marc walked slowly to Winger's house, apprehensive that Carrie had mentioned something to Winger. The smell of Cleo's cooking wafted toward him before he reached the back door. He suddenly realized he hadn't eaten since early this morning. He was starved. As usual, it was a super meal and Charlie gave his encore of raves, which Cleo took to heart, every savory word.

During the meal, Marc waited for some mention of the day, but nothing was said, and he sensed nothing unusual. Afterward, Charlie excused himself and took off for the bungalow. He had spent the entire day scouring the brush for stray cattle. He made no bones about being ready for bed.

Winger pushed back his chair and announced he wanted to watch a special news report. "Want to watch with me?" he asked Marc.

That was not the usual pattern, so Marc decided Winger wanted to discuss something with him. Here it is, he thought. Carrie had said something. "I'll be right in," Marc answered, but knew they would never talk during the news program. He turned to Cleo, who had already started to clear the table. "I'll give you a hand, Cleo."

She protested. "No, no. Go on in the front room."

But Marc said nothing, only began to help clear, scrape, and rinse while Cleo put food away and filled the dishwasher.

"Usually Winger helps," Cleo confided. "After you two are gone, he helps. My, it was a hot day. I bet it was hot at the fairgrounds, wasn't it?"

Marc couldn't help grinning. "Yes, it sure was hot." There was no response from Cleo as to his double meaning, so he knew Cleo had no knowledge of Carrie's flare-up. Well, that was a relief. Now for Winger.

Cleo chatted on, then chased Marc into the front room. "I'll be in there shortly," she told him.

A commercial blared, so Winger lowered the volume with his remote control. He was settled in an overstuffed easy chair with his long legs stretched out to a hassock, where only the high heels of his western boots rested. A toothpick shifted about in the corner of his mouth. His hair had been sandy in his youth and now gray was blending in. Whatever curls had cropped up in the thick, sandy top were flattened to a mere kink by the constant wearing of his large western hat.

"How was your day?" he asked, looking expectantly at Marc. "Going in again tomorrow?"

Marc nodded, and sat down on the sofa.

"When the news is over, let me hear how Carrie did today. Couldn't get much out of her, but I suspect it was not all that she wanted. Eh?" Then Winger saw that the commercial was over, and flicked the television back on.

Another nod was given, but Winger was already involved with the news. There was nothing to do but to watch and wait. Cleo came in and sank onto the sofa next to Marc.

Before Cleo had an opportunity to say a word, Winger, without breaking his concentration or gaze, said, "Cleo, honey, please don't talk during the news."

Marc suppressed a smile, but Cleo patted his arm and whispered, "He knows me so well." Then Marc smiled openly.

While the news rattled on, Marc reflected on the situation. For one thing, he was sure Carrie had not said a word about their difference. He stopped for a minute to listen to something on the news but it was only local news.

Back again to the details of the day. What would he tell Winger? If Carrie had said nothing, then he was free to choose. Her behavior during the drive into town and back was strange, even hostile. Her direct coolness told him at once where he belonged. Should he tell Winger that? The rudeness? That she treated him like a servant who had no right to speak to her? He could not understand her behavior. He had never met anyone like Carrie.

He could not understand Carrie in the context of her family. Warm. Easy to be with, friendly. They reached out to him, and Charlie, making them feel comfortable and at home. It was Carrie. She was the one who was aloof, unreachable.

Suddenly, before he realized, a wave of homesickness swept over him. It caught him short. He had felt he was past that sort of thing. Mature. But right now he missed his family. His grandparents, along with his three sisters and two brothers. There was always something happening in their home, but fun, mostly. His mother worked in Denver, and she came home on the weekends. His father had died when he was quite young, but his family stayed very close. What made the difference, he was sure, was the shortage of sisters and brothers. If Carrie had as many sisters as he had, things would always be jumping. How well he knew! He smiled now as he thought of them.

But Carrie did have a brother. That he had learned very abruptly. Wham! Like he had hit a brick wall. Sitting quietly, not showing any of the emotions that had so suddenly and fleetingly gripped him, he examined the pictures that covered the top of the old upright piano. There were more on the fireplace, and the end tables were well-decorated with them.

He studied the ones with the children. Two children, always. Carrie was, of course, the girl, and the boy had to be her brother. He was dark, like Mr. Courtley. The brown eyes, serious and deep, yet wide and eager. And there were horses. Lots of horses, with this brother on them, or beside them, holding ribbons or trophies. Yes, whoever this was, he was good with horses.

Where was he now? School? In the service? There were numerous possibilities. Dare he ask? He was never mentioned and that signaled caution for Marc. Perhaps Winger or Cleo would mention him in the course of casual talk.

Suddenly, there was silence. Winger had snapped off the television. "Well, that wasn't much of a special report. No rain, at least, and that's what's really important."

Cleo, who had set aside some crocheting to work at a large, thousand-piece puzzle on a card table, remarked, "We do know our congressman will visit the area this summer, and I, for one, want to see him."

"I'll see that you do," Winger promised.

"Marc, help me with this puzzle. A forest is bad enough, but that is a wheat field with mountains in the background. Ugh!"

"I need to talk with Marc about Carrie's riding. Don't get him sidetracked. What went wrong?" Winger asked directly.

Marc had decided to discuss riding only, and with that decision, he told Winger what he thought. "I think she's scared. She has competed before but not in this class. She needs work on the changing of gaits. It wasn't smooth and she knew it."

Winger scratched his head and took the toothpick from his mouth. "Scared. Broke her concentration. Mostly I thought, she was trying to compete instead of doing her best. If she were aiming at her best, she wouldn't break her concentration."

"Competing? I don't understand," Marc replied. "Of course, she was competing." He frowned.

Cleo clucked, "Now, now, now . . . she'll do all right." It was her defense of Carrie.

"Cleo, I need to know where and how to help the girl," Winger reminded her.

"I offered to help her, but . . ." Then Marc hesitated. Perhaps he should not have said that.

"But what?" Winger wanted to know, remembering her quick reaction to the same suggestion. Carrie could flare.

Marc knew he was on touchy ground. "Well, she really wasn't too happy with that idea," he put it gently. "In fact, she said her brother could help her better."

Cleo drew in her breath. She sought Winger's eyes, hers wide and a bit frightened. "Why, I've never heard Carrie talk like that!"

"Now, Cleo, you're aware of her feelings. That's why I said she's competing," Winger said quietly.

"Will he be here to help her train? She said he was really good," Marc asked. Enthusiasm filled his voice.

A strange silence followed. Another alarmed eye signal flew between Winger and Cleo.

"Oh, dear," Cleo finally managed. For once she appeared speechless.

Before either of them had an opportunity to speak further, someone knocked on the door. Cleo leaped in relief to answer it. It was a neighbor. "Why, Curtis, come in," Cleo greeted warmly. "Look here, Winger, it's Curtis."

In his easy way, Winger rose slowly from his chair to shake hands with his neighbor. The entire atmosphere changed from an embarrassed lull to a chattery friendliness that swept away the earlier conversation. It was done, closed, and Marc was still left wondering when this brother would be back, or from where at least.

"Sit down, Curtis. I'll make some coffee. And

cake? Of course. I know you." Cleo pattered on, clearly not speechless anymore as she whizzed off into the kitchen.

"No sense in saying no, Curtis. Sit down," Winger laughed, but before he did so, Winger introduced him to Marc.

"Hello," Marc said, greeting him with a firm handshake. Then he said to Winger, "I think I'll leave now. I've got to be up early tomorrow."

"Thanks for your help, Marc," Winger told him and waved.

Marc called good-bye to Cleo in the kitchen, and left by the front door.

It was dusk. The softness of the approaching night moved slowly out of the east, while the lingering day followed the sun westward. Birds twittered and fluttered among the cover of leaves, settling and resettling before the final curtain of night. Marc breathed deeply. He cherished this land where some of his ancestors could be traced into the centuries past. It tied him to the land in a special way.

He sat on an old cottonwood tree stump near the bungalow to mingle with the coming of night. He thought of his mother in Denver amidst the hurry and noise of the city. He had an impulse to call her, but no, he'd work this out on his own. Marc was sure that Carrie hated him. But why? And what about her brother? Why did she bring him up so suddenly out of the clear blue? And boy, Winger and Cleo reacted strongly to something he had said. What was this strange gift he seemed to have of late? He spoke, and presto, a peculiar silence immediately filled the room. But what in the world had he said?

And what had he said that first night on the ranch? This was more than Carrie's shyness. Her parents had been startled, too. Horses. He had been talking to Carrie about horses. His horse, Fleeting Cloud. He had said she was a mustang. Then silence, awkward silence. Now tonight, horses; but also a brother. So it had to do with horses and a mysterious brother.

Perhaps the brother was estranged from his family for some reason. It happens. His uncle had argued with his grandfather years ago over a matter no one could pinpoint anymore and had not spoken to the family for twenty years. Maybe this was the case here.

Regardless, Carrie's brother was somewhere, but from now on he knew enough to be quiet. It was not his business, and he was not about to have Carrie turn that rudeness on him again. As he sat thinking of Carrie, her family, and Winger and Cleo, there was something that bothered him. Deep down he knew Carrie was not a rude person. Maybe shy, unsure of herself, but not rude.

It was dark. The weariness of the day tugged at him. Best to shower, sleep, and be ready for whatever tomorrow had in store. He rose and went inside.

The following day proved as fruitless for Carrie as the first, and it was no better on the third. She didn't win; she didn't have high placings.

Whatever feelings she had, Carrie kept to herself, and Marc silently drove her back and forth. He was secretly delighted when the horse show was over, and he hoped Mr. Courtley would not ask him again. He did feel sorry for Carrie, as all of her high hopes seemed dashed to the ground. Now, she'd have to work at her training, but also build up her courage and strength to go on. She was not a quitter, but Marc wished he could encourage and comfort her a little.

For the remainder of the week he worked with Charlie on numerous jobs that kept him away from the ranch buildings, so he had no idea what was taking place in the corral, nor did he ask Winger.

Sunday was his day off. Mr. Courtley never invaded the privacy of their day off. There wasn't enough time to go home. Besides, he did not want to spend his money on travel when he needed it so desperately this fall at the university.

This Sunday, after speaking with his grandparents and mother, he decided to ride one of the ranch horses. Riding over the countryside would ease the strain of this peculiar week. He wished he could have Fleeting Cloud to ride, but that would have to wait.

The Courtley ranch had about twenty horses grazing in a back pasture, the number changing as mares foaled, or as horses were bought and sold. This pasture is where Marc headed with the jeep. He singled out a beautiful chestnut gelding, and had no difficulty luring the horse with a bucket containing a small amount of oats.

Only too willingly the horse followed, eager for the treat on the bottom of the bucket. After being haltered, he got his treat and Marc led him back to the barn behind the jeep.

Soon he was heading up the hill behind the house, gliding with the power of this magnificent creature. Oh, what a horse! Marc felt the spirit of the animal at once. The horse must have felt a kindred spirit, for they seemed to immediately blend together as one moving entity. He rode bareback, which made him feel even more a part of the horse. Only a blanket and bridle adorned the chestnut.

Halfway up the hill, Marc reined to a stop. Before him spread a sweeping view; a symphony of color, texture, and space. The deep blue of the sky held a few white puffy clouds which shadowed upon the gold and green prairie that spread to meet the eastern horizon. The roads ran like the warp and woof of a giant patchwork quilt. Closer, he gazed down upon the black roofs of the ranch buildings. It was then that he spotted Carrie and her mother climbing the hill carrying something in a basket. They appeared to be heading toward a small stand of pine trees about a fourth of the way up the hill. A picnic? It was a beautiful day for one. He hoped Carrie was in better spirits than on the days of her defeats.

It occurred to him that he did not want Carrie to see him watching, as it may be interpreted as snooping. He sped to the summit and over the top. "Well, whatever your name is," he said to the horse, "we had better be on our way." A good nudge sent the horse flying upward once more.

When Marc returned in the late afternoon, he galloped back over the top and down the hill, his mind once again at ease. Coming down, his path was not exactly the same as when he rode up, and this time he passed the pines. Surely Carrie and her mother were no longer there, so he stopped to enjoy the pines himself. He slid off the chestnut's back and walked, leading the horse. The smell of pines engulfed him as he wound himself among the evergreens. Even the slightest breeze played on the millions of needles, creating its own music. The enjoyment was shortened when he discovered what was in the center of the group of pines, and once again he felt like the intruder.

There in front of him was a well-tended family cemetery surrounded by an old, fancy iron fence. There were quite a few headstones, eight, nine, all of course with the name Courtley. The dates told the story. The Courtleys had been on the land a long time.

"Here we will not stay," Marc told the horse. "This is what is known as private." The horse snickered.

Marc had just pulled the reins to lead the horse out of the pines when his attention was drawn to fresh flowers on one of the graves. Funny, he thought. Surely, the Courtleys have been here a long time. Why flowers, and why on only one of the graves? Scanning the headstone, a strange tingly sensation ran up his back until it hit his brain with an impact. His breathing became shallow and short.

Allen James Courtley V
1960–1976
Our
beloved
son and brother

A dullness hit the pit of his stomach. He had no idea! Thoughts and scenes of the past weeks tumbled about into place, and it all synthesized. Carrie's brother was dead!

Why hadn't they just said so? That was the last thing that would ever have occurred to him. Dead! So young! He was stunned. Obviously Carrie and her mother were carrying flowers in the basket earlier that day.

He shifted his weight from one foot to the other, at the same time removing his hat, his dark hair blending with the gathering shadows in the clustering trees.

"What are you doing here?" a voice demanded.

Marc darted as if struck by an ancient arrow. He spun about to find himself staring at Carrie.

SEVEN

CARRIE stood only a foot or so from him. Her thick hair hung free, and the blue of her blouse matched the blue of her eyes, which at this moment were as hard as nails. Being tiny, she barely came to his shoulder and had to tilt her head up to look straight into Marc's eyes.

Still shaken from the sudden realization, Marc's immediate response was one of compassion. "Carrie," he timidly began.

But while Marc was overwhelmed with newfound compassion, Carrie still viewed him as an intruder. And one that had gone too far, encroaching upon the sanctuary she cherished most. She stood, looking at him defiantly.

"Why are you here, and why are you riding my brother's horse?" she demaned.

"Your brother's?!" Marc was stunned again. Would he ever do anything right?"

"Yes, Character is my brother's horse," she abruptly informed him.

Marc's compassion turned to quick defense. Her expression had not changed. "Well, Carrie,

I simply chose a horse from the back pasture. Your father said to just take any one, so I did. I had no idea about your brother, or his horse," Marc tried to explain.

A cold stare was his answer.

"Carrie," Marc tried again, desperately. "Please listen. I am not snooping. I rode down off the hill and came through the trees not knowing this was the family cemetery." He hesitated. Carrie was unmoved. Then a spark of anger flamed. Why was he trying to explain anything to her? Only a hateful glare met his words, then he added with firmness, "I offend you no matter what I do or say, Carrie. I think it is best that you and I avoid each other. We just do not understand one another and it causes nothing but tension." He spoke, looking directly at her.

Carrie flinched. She had not expected that, and it took away her thunder, leaving her without much to say except a hurried, "All right."

Exasperated, Marc leaped lightly unto the horse, swung his head in the direction of the barn, and rode off through the trees, Sensing that Carrie had turned to watch him, he cast a quick glance over his shoulder. He was right.

Standing there in the gathering twilight, Carrie felt suddenly empty. She watched until the trees shut Marc from her view. With all her heart, she wished she hadn't spoken as she had, and yet it had rankled deeply that she had found him there. But the hurt in his eyes had been evident. He truly had not known about Allen or the cemetery.

She sighed deeply and sank to the ground. An evening breeze sent a chorus of whispers through the pines, as if sighing with her. She was sure he had not told anyone about how rudely she had treated him during those three days going to and from the horse show. She had wondered about that, and looking in the direction that Marc had taken, she knew just as certainly that he would not mention this encounter.

If Marc had said anything to her father, or anyone, but especially her father, he would have come down hard on her. He would not tolerate the ranch help being treated unkindly; or worse still, subserviently. She had done that to Marc. She had done it with her rude silence and curt, short answers, and she had done it just now with her demanding attitude. If Marc had been out of place toward her that would have been taken care of also . . . by her father, not by Carrie. Cleo was right, of course — Marc Bear was a fine person, and he had just laid the ground rules: avoid each other. That would be for the rest of the summer. Well, that would suit her fine.

But she turned and whispered, as if Allen could hear her speak. "What am I going to do, Allen? I don't like any of this. I don't like to see him on your horse and every time I see him, I think of you. You should be here, not Marc."

Her gloom matched that which was closing around her. Then, she added sadly, "I'm in trouble with my riding, Allen. People expect me to be as good as you were, and I want to be . . . but I'm not."

Carrie got up and trudged down the slope to the house. She did not see Marc the next day while she trained in the corral. True to his word, he stayed out of her sight. She now had her way, and it should have made her happy but it didn't.

Winger trained her with a fury now. He had only an hour or so to give of his time and the rest was up to Carrie. After a week of this, and little progress, Carrie was disgusted. Then when Winger announced that he could not help her at all because there was too much work to do on the ranch, she sank to an all-time low.

"But Winger, that's not fair!" Carrie protested.

Winger laughed. "Fair? I'll say it isn't fair. It isn't fair that I have all that work!"

They were in the corral. Winger was sitting on the fence and Carrie on Morning Star. The session was over, at least Winger's part. Carrie still had the rest of the morning to work out. A few crows cawed from the nearby cottonwoods as if to protest with Carrie.

"What am I going to do?" Carrie asked with a face like a cloudy day.

"Well, there will be an answer. I think I have one, if you'll listen," Winger told her. His gray eyes gazed steadily from beneath the wide brim of the western hat, and his look was thoughtful, as if carefully weighing what he would say next.

Carrie stared back. What answer could he possibly have? This was ruining her summer plans . . . completely. First Barney. Now Winger. Things weren't right at all. Disappointment registered not only on her face, but in the slump of her body as she sat there staring into Winger's gray eyes.

Slowly, he began, "Kitten, why don't you let Marc help you? Now, don't look like that! I tell you he's good. I've seen him ride, and I know after pulling it out of him that he has won many a ribbon . . . like Allen. His grandfather taught him to ride. That side of the family is Comanche and horses were second nature to them."

"I don't care if he rides elephants. No, no, no!" she emphasized through clenched teeth.

Morning Star twitched her ears.

A twinkle flickered in Winger's eyes. "Now, don't go scaring your horse." Then more gently, "You are going to have to work this out with your dad. You would let Allen help you if he were here. Think of Marc as a brother."

"He is not Allen! He is not my brother!" Carrie was adamant.

"Your brother wouldn't like the way you're acting right now," Winger reminded her with a touch of sternness.

That hit the mark. She started.

"You think a bit, Kitten," Winger counseled. "Now I've got to run." He jumped down off the fence and strode toward the barn. Soon he headed out in his pickup, leaving a trail of dust to mingle with the fading roar of the engine. Then it was still; even the crows had decided to hush or leave. No, there they were, circling.

Carrie sat, just she and the crows. Absolutely everyone else on the ranch was gone, even Cleo. It was nine-fifteen, still early, and she had lots of work to do. Yet she didn't move. Morning Star stomped her impatience and the sun beat its unrelenting reminder on her western hat, of just how hot it was.

Everything was a mess! This was supposed to be the best summer ever, and now her eager expectations were not just drooping, but wilting, fading, one by one. What was happening? She had a week and a half until the next show.

Covering her eyes with one hand as if to think, she decided suddenly to chuck the whole thing for the day. Debbie was coming over to spend the night because her parents had gone on an unexpected trip. Debbie said she would be there between one and two o'clock. "I'm going to go in and bake us some cookies, and that is that. Chocolate chip cookies!" Carrie yelled to the circling crows. As if they understood, they cawed back at her.

She rode Morning Star into the barn, and while she slipped off the saddle and bridle Carrie confided in her best listener. "Now, none of this is your fault, you understand? It's all mine. So I don't want you getting a complex." She pulled the blanket off and threw it over the stall divider. "You let me do that."

Morning Star, not the least concerned about anything other than getting her regular oats and a run in the pasture, rolled her eyes and shook her head, rippling her white, silky mane.

"Knew you'd understand," and with that, Carrie gave her an extra pat, then led her out of the barn and across the wide driveway to the fenced pasture on the other side.

The rest of the morning was spent baking and in the afternoon when Debbie arrived, they rode horses, but only for pleasure. They didn't even discuss shows or training. Supper turned out to be really fun. Carrie was glad Debbie had come. She had a way of seeing the funny side of just about anything. All of Carrie's worries faded momentarily as they all sat around the table for dinner.

Debbie was a decided contrast to Carrie, tall, thin, to the point that some would call skinny. She had deep brown eyes, which seemed a paradox to her very blond, curly hair, which she wore short. A ready smile was her trademark. Debbie's nature was outgoing, open, another contrast to the introspective Carrie, but the friendship had begun years ago, regardless of the differences, and had endured.

"Debbie, it's so good to see you again," Mrs. Courtley said as she began passing the food. "I'll always remember your laughter interrupting my English class."

"Well, Mrs. Courtley, it wasn't my fault that I laughed so much," Debbie reminded her. "It was that Joe Lucas. He's been in a lot of my classes, and he always makes me laugh."

"Yes, I know," Mrs. Courtley agreed. "Even the teachers enjoy his humor."

Debbie giggled. "Remember that time he played Lady Macbeth when so many girls were out with the flu?" Then she proceeded to imitate him.

"Stop it, Debbie. I can't eat and laugh, too," Carrie said, trying not to laugh.

"You know who he is, Carrie, so you know what he did in that class," Debbie said.

Carrie nodded.

Mr. Courtley asked Debbie, "What are you going to major in at the university? You would be a terrific actress."

"No, I'm going into civil engineering," she answered.

"Civil engineering?" Mr. Courtley replied, surprised.

"You haven't changed your mind about that, have you?" Mrs. Courtley declared. "My, that surely seemed to upset the boys when you read your 'I want to be . . .' paper."

"They did have a good time with that, didn't they," Debbie recalled. "Well, I haven't changed my mind at all."

"I'm going to miss you next year," Carrie sighed.

"Hey! I'm not gone yet," Debbie reminded her.

They ate the rest of the meal quietly. Everything concerned with Marc and riding was in another world. The subject never came up, and only when Debbie decided to take a second piece of chocolate cake did the word riding enter into the conversation at all.

"Debbie sure doesn't have to worry about ask him for help. Right now she would rather weight. A second piece of cake will make no difference to her at all," Mrs. Courtley said, re-filling her plate.

"Well, if I ever put on weight, which I doubt, it would send Tumbleweed into a state of shock. He's used to me sitting thin in the saddle for three years now." Then she added, "Mrs. Courtley, let Carrie and me do the dishes."

"Gladly," Mrs. Courtley answered. "Have a good visit." Then she and Mr. Courtley rose to go into the front room. As they went through the shuttered swinging doors, Mrs. Courtley turned to Debbie. "If you want to stay longer than just tonight with your parents gone, feel free."

"Thanks," Debbie answered.

Alone in the kitchen they proceeded to clear the table when Carrie blurted, "Oooops! I forgot to ask Dad something important. Be right back."

She scooted into the front room, then reappeared shortly through the swinging doors. She looked disgusted.

Debbie was sure she knew what the problem was. "You and that horse! Now what?"

"Oh, let's not even talk about it," Carrie groaned, then added anyway, "Winger can't help me anymore and you know that I need help!"

"I'm working out with John because Barney is gone. Want to come over?" Debbie offered.

"I know you're riding with John, but I'd have to travel too far. You're closer. It's no problem for you."

"What did Winger say?" Debbie asked.

"Oh, that I had to work it out with Dad, and Dad says that *I* have to work it out," Carrie answered.

"Well?" Debbie asked again, and gave her the high-eyebrow look.

"Well what?" Carrie demanded. "You're as bad as the others."

"Your big problem is you, Carrie," Debbie said, not unkindly.

"That is just what I told Morning Star this morning." Carrie laughed. "I am the one with the complex."

"Well, at least you've let the horse off the hook. Be serious now, Carrie," Debbie continued, "you know the trouble. You want to ride exactly like Allen."

Carrie shut off the water and grabbed a towel to dry her hands. "Why shouldn't I, Deb? Why not? People expect it! You heard them at the last show. We discussed it then and things haven't changed. 'Not brilliant like her brother!' 'She'll never match her brother!' Blah, blah, blah. Winger tells me the same thing and then there's that Marc Bear!" Carrie spilled out with untempered vigor.

"Marc Bear? What does he had to do with anything?" Debbie wanted to know. She shut the dishwasher. "He's only here for the summer."

"Come on, let's go up to my room," Carrie hurriedly said, avoiding the last comment. That had slipped out, and the last thing she wanted to discuss was Marc Bear, especially since she had to shut him out. She gave the sink another wipe for good measure. "Want anything more to eat?" she asked Debbie.

"Are you kidding?" Debbie groaned, holding her stomach.

"Just thought I'd ask," Carrie replied. "No guest goes hungry in the Courtley place."

They drifted through the front room and up the stairs. When finally bathed, with hair washed and blown dry and in pajamas, they each settled on a twin bed.

"I hate to think of your being gone next year," Carrie complained. She sat on the bed winding her hair into one long braid.

Debbie gathered the extra throw pillows that were on the usually made twin bed and stacked them in a pile, then sank back into them. Her short, curly hair was like a blond misty halo about her head. "Oh, you'll follow the year after. You won't get rid of me that easy." She shifted so she could see Carrie better. "Now, you tell me what this Marc Bear has to do with anything. You won't introduce him to any of us . . . is he human, this mystery person? And, most of all, why does he bother you?"

"He doesn't bother me!" Carrie answered curtly.

"Humph! He does so," Debbie insisted.

"Well, I didn't introduce him that day at the show because you, well, not you, but John and Kathy were saying all that stupid stuff. Just like you're saying now."

Debbie sat up. "Do you like him, Caroline Courtley?"

"Like him?!" Carrie exploded. "I wish he would vanish."

Nestling back in her pile of pillows, Debbie turned her head, a smirk on her face. "Carrie!" she sang.

"Honest Deb, he's a pain." Then she immediately regretted the comment. She bit her lip and added, "Well, not really that."

Actually, not having seen Marc for a while, she realized she missed him. Even though Marc triggered off memories of her brother whenever she had seen him, she now missed those fleeting glimpses. It confused her, and made her more determined to shut him out as much as possible.

She told Debbie, "He irritates me . . . really bugs me every time we cross paths. Last week I found him up in the cemetery. That really got me and I told him so. He didn't know about Allen, or the cemetery; he just happened to ride into the pines, but it upset me. Then he became angry and said we should avoid each other. I hurt his feelings. I know it. Boy, if Dad knew that, he would skin me alive."

Debbie giggled. "That bad?"

"It's not funny!" came Carrie's quick retort.

She sat quietly, her chin resting on her raised knees. Debbie gazed gently at her friend from her mountain of pillows. She knew Carrie had feelings to work out because of her brother, but being an observer gave her a view Carrie didn't have.

"Let's not talk about him," Carrie finally said. "I don't know what to think. First I see him riding Allen's horse. Then, his horse is half mustang and my dad calls him son. Now Winger says he's qualified to train me, and Dad agrees. If I want to ride and train, I have to ask him to help me."

"So ask him," Debbie told her. "You're making too much of this, Carrie. He will never take Allen's place. How could you imagine such a thing?"

"But Allen was . . ." Then Carrie stopped. "And Marc brings back all sorts of memories I would rather forget."

"I know," Debbie sympathized. "I don't really truly know, but I can understand a little."

"He'll be gone at the end of the summer anyway," Carrie said. "He's going to the University of Colorado, same as you. Let's get some sleep. And thanks for talking about it, Deb. Think you'll stay longer?"

They climbed under the covers. Debbie shoved all the pillows onto the floor and snapped off the light. "I don't know," she said. "My mom will call home tomorrow. Good night, Carrie. Everything will be fine. Marc will help you, I'm sure."

"Good night," Carrie answered, but she didn't go to sleep right away. She wasn't as sure as Debbie that Marc would help her at all. How would she approach him? And maybe he would refuse. He had that right. Her father would not insist that he do it. Plus, her father had no inkling as to her extreme sensitivity toward Marc. But Winger did, and he was ashamed of her behavior in the matter. If she kept it up, her father would find out and she'd have to explain.

She looked over at her friend. Debbie was already asleep. Debbie was objective, even adding her good humor. Carrie, on the other hand, saw no humor in this at all. After some time Carrie drifted to sleep, leaving her thoughts to the next day.

Debbie stayed until noon, then whirled off in a cloud of dust, to pick up her parents at the airport seventy-five miles away.

Carrie didn't ride after Debbie left or even go near the horse, but she left Morning Star in the pasture to run. All of the men had left before dawn. Sometime in July the branding would start, and all of the stray cattle had to be driven out of the arroyos and brush. The Black Angus could not easily be hidden for too long since their color betrays them against the brown and green of the terrain.

Her mother was gone, too. She had signed up for a university class that was being held in the Prairie View High School, and that is where she would be every morning until the end of July.

Alone. That described her day once Debbie had sped out of sight. Cleo was at home, but Carrie preferred being alone just now, and stayed in her room. She picked up a half-finished book, but she found herself going over the same sentence again and again without absorbing the words or meaning. What went on in her head as she sat on her bed holding her book was how she would approach Marc and ask for his help. Her father had made it clear that she would have to do the asking, and that she had to decide if she even wanted to continue to go the competitions at all. Well, she knew she couldn't quit.

Now, in her mind's eye she rehearsed what she would say to Marc; then she changed it, then again, and then again. What if he refused? How would she react to that? Tears? Pleading? Anger? Silence?

The day dragged forever. Once in a while she would watch Morning Star from her bedroom window, then she'd gaze back toward the hills. She wondered how far back into the hills the men had gone. Far enough to see the mustangs, or at least get a glimpse of them. She didn't think so. That was quite a ways back. No one bothered the wild horses on the Courtley spread, and in time the intelligent creatures learned where safety lay. Would that black-devil mare still be parading the hills with the band? No one had seen her in the four years since she had fled over the fence. Maybe she had not even made it back into the hills.

About four o'clock her mother returned, then at five-thirty, the men. Carrie knew she could not go to the adobe bungalow. That was not allowed. So she had to see Marc while he was with Cleo and Winger or working somewhere around the ranch buildings. The thought of asking him in front of others gave her chills, since she had to humble herself anyway. That isn't what she wanted, so she had to find Marc alone, somewhere. That might prove more difficult than it seemed. She stood at her window watching the men come and go, then it happened. Winger and Charlie headed for the house, and Marc was going into the barn. Alone!

Racing down the stairs she flew through the kitchen. Her mother looked up, startled. "Whoa! Where is the race?"

"Be back in a minute, Mom. I'll help with supper," she yelled, then continued on her flight.

Bonnie Lass leaped off the porch to join the run. But by the corner of the corral, Carrie skidded to a full stop. No way did she want to be seen running into the barn — not by Marc Bear, anyway. She deliberately walked step by slow step into the barn. She hated it, but if she wanted his expertise, she'd have to set her feelings aside and work with him . . . if he would do it.

Her eyes adjusted to the gloomy interior. There he was! He was standing by the machinery with his back toward her. Carrie could hear her heart pounding in her ears. This was so dumb! Why should she be scared? Why did he do this to her?

"Marc?" she called in a small voice. He didn't hear her.

Louder she called again. "Marc?"

This time he turned his head.

"Marc, could I talk with you for a minute?" she asked hesitatntly.

There was no answer but he walked toward her. Finally he was standing close to her, looking down. His face showed nothing, his eyes masked with indifference. He wore no hat, and his dark hair softened his rugged features.

"What do you want?" he asked in a soft voice, but one directed toward business.

Being uneasy, she shifted from one foot to the other and cleared her throat. "Well . . ." And then she raised her eyes to his.

All sorts of little butterflies began to flutter about inside, and she knew she blushed. She always did. She was grateful the dim barn would hide it. His once only interesting face, was suddenly handsome but also cold and distant.

She rushed on. "Winger can't help me train anymore, and he says that you're very good. Would you help me?"

Marc could see how difficult this was for her, and although he had a sense of tenderness as she stood there humbling herself, he stood just as firmly in his intended aloofness. He wouldn't open himself to being hurt again.

"I'll help you, of course," he responded carefully. "Your dad wants me to work on the machinery before the harvest so I'll be here in the barn a good share of the time. How about three hours a day . . . but Carrie, it's all business. Is that understood?"

He'd help! She drew a deep breath. Her world was back in order again and running. "That's fine," she agreed.

Then, without thinking, she reached out and touched his arm. It startled her — and Marc. Their eyes met briefly in disbelief. Carrie was instantly flustered. She spun about and ran back to the house.

EIGHT

*T*HEY began early. By ten o'clock they had put in their agreed three hours, which was strictly trainer-student and more austere than even Carrie had thought. There was no smalltalk or reference to anything but the issue at hand: training a horse and rider. Marc perched himself on the fence and barked his orders, then when he saw something that needed correcting, he'd jump off and run to the center of the corral or run along aside Carrie, still shouting his instructions. His eyes never left Carrie and the horse.

When it was all over, it was clear that Marc was bothered, not pleased with something. It showed in his voice when he called Carrie to him as he perched on the fence again. He reached out to pat Morning Star on the neck and scratched her behind the ears as the horse came close to him.

"What is it?" Carrie wanted to know. She didn't look directly at Marc but past him.

Marc was definitely the authority here. There was no question or hesitation in his manner as he confronted Carrie. He stared at Carrie, not saying a word until she finally brought her eyes into contact with his. They were so close they could easily have touched. Carrie braced herself inside and stared back with the same intensity with which he stared at her. He wasn't just staring, he was studying her.

He finally spoke. "Carrie, I am going to ask you a question and I want a frank answer. It's important. What do you think when you are riding? Your concentration is not with the horse, and I need to know why." His voice was filled with soft authority. It was this self-assurance that Carrie thought was arrogance when they had first met.

Carrie shifted her gaze into the distance as she spoke. "Well, I think of how I am sitting, the timing of the gaits, transition and . . ." Then, as Carrie drew her attention back to Marc, she could see these were not the right answers. He was shaking his head. "What else is there?" she demanded smartly.

Without taking his gaze from her face, he said, "My grandfather taught me to ride and the first thing that he ever told me, was this — that the spirit of the horse and rider must be one. It is necessary, or there is no communication. If you do not have this communication you will not flow with the movement of the horse." He spoke with a quiet importance.

Carrie nodded, yet protested. "Are you saying that Morning Star and I don't communicate? Are you telling me this is what is wrong?" She clearly showed her disbelief, tinged with disgust.

Without a word, Marc affirmed her conclusion. The protest continued, yet Carrie stayed calm.

She was not about to lose control, so, with words that came out in steely firmness, she stated, "I've had this horse since she was a colt. No one else has handled her. How could I not communicate with her?"

Marc didn't budge from his position, either on the fence or from his conclusion. Carrie hadn't given him the answers that would uncover the reasons for her lack of oneness in moving with the horse, so there was nothing he could do but wait until she realized it herself.

Neither of them spoke. The impasse sat with intense stillness between them. It was a strange, silent battle. Marc continued to gaze intently into Carrie's eyes. He didn't flinch for a second, and Carrie, for once determined that she would not fluster and blush, returned the steady gaze.

It was Carrie who spoke again. "You didn't tell me how it is that Morning Star and I don't communicate," she challenged.

"That is the mystery," Marc answered. "Why aren't you and the horse moving as one? You tell me." And with that, he jumped down off the fence. Then he smiled up at her, his eyes warm and friendly. "See you tomorrow at the same time," he said, giving Morning Star an extra pat.

In utter frustration Carrie stared after him as he walked off in the direction of Winger's house with that same easy, assured gait.

"Did you hear that? Boy, does he have his nerve, especially when he doesn't even know what he is talking about!"

Later that evening as she sat in the front room

with her father, she told him what Marc had said, then added, "Doesn't that seem strange to you? Talking about spirits like that? And I mean, who else would know Morning Star? Who? He doesn't make sense!"

Supper was over, and they were watching the evening news. Mrs. Courtley sat in the small office doing her homework for her class. Carrie sat on the couch with her father. She needed to talk because she didn't know how she was going to work with Marc. Really! Her father would surely understand that he was off-base.

But to her surprise her father answered, "Well, I don't know. I think he is speaking in terms of his heritage, but any horseman would understand what he is talking about."

"Dad!" Carrie exclaimed, shocked.

"Now, Carrie, he's speaking about that special combination of horse and rider. Call it spirits or whatever you like," her father said. "But he is right, it has to be there."

Carrie couldn't believe her ears. She sat straight up, facing her father. "What are you saying? That you agree with him? That I don't know Morning Star?!" Her eyes widened as she spoke. This was too much!

Her mother, hearing the raised voices, came from the office. She came to the sofa. Yes, her daughter was about to explode like a time bomb. She sat in a chair opposite the sofa. Carrie turned a desperate look for help in her direction. If her mother took Marc's side . . . well, she would not work with him at all. That was final.

"Mother?" Carrie began, the desperation showing in her voice.

Her mother and father exchanged glances.

"Are you going to take his side?" Carrie asked after seeing them look at each other.

Her mother spoke softly. "Carrie, there are no sides here. It is a matter of understanding."

"What is there to understand?" Carrie demanded. "Marc said I don't know my own horse. How can he teach me to ride when he says things like that?"

Carefully her mother asked, "How did Marc put it?"

Carrie remembered well enough, so she answered sarcastically. "Our spirits are not one," she mimicked.

Mr. Courtley lowered his head as if to suppress a smile, but Mrs. Courtley remained intently quiet before attempting to answer because she knew what she said would make a big difference in how Carrie reacted.

"Now, Carrie, will you listen to me, quietly, because I want you to think about what I am going to say before you react," her mother asked.

Carrie nodded.

"I believe that Marc has struck at the heart of something. In many ways we have been trying to tell you the same thing, only we have been indirect. Marc has not wasted his time on that but has put it bluntly . . . and, it's made you mad. He doesn't care about that. You asked for his help, and he is going to give it as he sees it," her mother said plainly.

"Well, that is a big help. Some help!" Carrie blurted.

Her mother continued. "What Marc is saying, is that something is coming between you and the horse. It doesn't make any difference how long you've had Morning Star . . . that isn't it. And I think you know full well what the problem is. Your brother."

"Mother! How can you say that!" Carrie cried in utter dismay.

"I say it because it's true. You are not riding that horse with your spirit, if you want to put it that way," her mother said softly.

Carrie sat stunned. Her world was beginning to crumble. "But Allen rode so beautifully."

"Of course he did." Mrs. Courtley continued to make her point. Mr. Courtley nodded his encouragement. "There is a difference, Carrie, between perfecting your skill as a horsewoman, and perhaps riding as well as your brother, but not *as* your brother. You can not sit astride your horse as if you were Allen. *Your* spirit must prevail. This is the communication."

Carrie remained quiet for some time, along with her parents. Each seemed lost in thought, sorting things out. The grandfather clock chimed as if it was announcing the time for Carrie to awake and see what was true instead of being buried in a dream.

When Carrie spoke it was in hushed tones, as if the truth voiced too loudly would hurt her ears. "What a fine line," she whispered. "Marc asked me what I thought when I was riding . . .

and I think of Allen. If I were Allen, how would he do this or that?"

"I'd say that Marc Bear is a very unusual young man," her father said. "He knows nothing of your brother — that I am aware of anyhow."

A dart of guilt hit Carrie. "No, he knows nothing other than that Allen rode very well," she answered wistfully, remembering only too keenly the encounter in the cemetery.

She smiled at her mom, and gave her dad's hand a squeeze. "Well, now I have lots to think about, don't I? I'm going to my room. I'm all right."

As she rose, her mom and dad got up also to hug her. Carrie went slowly up the stairs to retreat to the sanctuary of her room, and there to think. She plopped flat on her bed and stared at the ceiling.

Her brother! Her idol and hero. The memory was now the only reality, and that could be built to any height. Her excessive attachment to the memory, had gone undetected until the substantial flesh reality of Marc Bear had been thrust, however unintentionally, on the scene. He had pierced the dream, and Carrie had fought back with the full depth of every emotion. She didn't want to let go of her brother. No! Then there were those other feelings she had toward Marc. They surfaced suddenly at unguarded moments when she came upon him unexpectantly, or when she saw him in the distance. The way he moved and stood, his quiet calmness, the depth of his eyes — they all bothered her. She wanted to see him and missed him when she didn't, and the same time, she wished he had never come to the ranch. She didn't need or even want him as a brother; but what then? Had Debbie struck at the truth? Did she really like Marc Bear?

Also, she was being forced by the ruthless fact that if she wanted to continue showmanship riding, and place, she would have to relinquish the very hero she wished to emulate. Her brother! What a paradox! How could she let go of this brother that she loved so much? And how had Marc perceived all of this?

Everything surged about inside. The tears flowed. There was angry protest. There was pity and sorrow, but mostly there was determination. One conclusion she did reach; Marc Bear was not going to know he was right. When the summer was over, he'd be gone. Things would return to normal.

After several hours of this tug-of-war she got ready for bed. About ten, her mother stuck her head in to say good night, but even when she had settled under the covers waiting for sleep, it didn't happen. She lay there tossing and turning until about midnight, then finally she fell into a fitful rest.

Seven o'clock found her on Morning Star, ready; she had figured out what she would do. Her brother would not enter into the business of her training. Not once. She would ride well, but as herself, so that Allen would be proud if he had lived to see her. That was one thing, and the other, she had promised herself that Marc would not know why he had been right.

Marc swung himself lightly up onto the fence. He gave easy, matter-of-fact instructions, making no reference to their battle of the wills of the day before.

Carrie listened carefully. When he was finished, she threw him a challenge. "Why don't you ride yourself and show me?"

After all, she had never seen him ride, not show style anyway. She'd put him on the spot for a change.

The challenge was met, but not as she expected.

"I'll ride," he answered, "but not on Morning Star. She must be accustomed to your command alone. I'll ride the chestnut after we are through practicing."

He meant Character! He was still in the front pasture across the way. She disliked seeing Marc ride that horse, but she herself had set this up and now there was no choice. She hid her disapproval.

After several hours of concentrated practice, Carrie began to witness the result of her determined effort. Marc, from his perch, nodded and displayed a brief smile from time to time. Yet he said nothing. He climbed down after an hour of practice and headed for the pasture. While Carrie continued on in the corral, he led Character into the barn and bridled him, then rode him through the gate into the corral.

Carrie was surprised. He used no saddle. "Why no saddle?" she called. She slipped off Morning Star and onto the fence to watch. Not having really worked with Character, Marc was at a disadvantage. Regardless of this, he went through the various gaits smoothly. He never answered her question about the saddle, but rode, while Character responded to every touch, seeming to remember everything Allen had taught him over four years ago. It was amazing.

Carrie could hardly believe it, and she was secretly impressed — very impressed. Winger had been right. When he was through, he simply rode the horse out of the corral, not giving her a chance to comment one way or the other. As far as Marc was concerned, he knew he was being held in comparison to her brother. It was left right there. He didn't come back to the corral after Character was put in the pasture but went straight to his work, and neither of them ever mentioned it again during the practice sessions.

Carrie's progress improved. It was obvious to everyone, and she began to experience a freedom in her riding she had not thought possible. Along with this, came an unconscious admiration for Marc. So it went, they were together for three hours a day, then they each went separate ways, avoiding each other.

Late in June Carrie had her second show. It was not a major one, although important to Carrie. Much to her relief, and Marc's, Winger drove her. The high placings she received were proof of her hard work and growing ability to ride as her own person. It pleased Carrie greatly, but she aimed higher still. She came back more determined than ever and worked twice as hard.

Then in the middle of July came a break in the routine of the ranch. Mr. Courtley took Carrie a hundred miles to the horse show in Harrisville. They'd be gone three to four days depending on the outcome of the first day. Marc, as usual, stayed out of view while they prepared to leave. He headed out at dawn for the north range.

But Carrie looked for him as they were ready to leave. This was a big show, important, and, well, she just thought he would be here to see her off but he wasn't. Winger caught the searching looks and remarked casually, "He's out on the north range, Kitten."

A quick blush revealed the truth of Winger's observation, but Carrie avoided his smile, embarrassed at having been seen actually looking for Marc. Yet, she was disappointed.

After Mr. Courtley had left with Carrie, Winger and Cleo left also, for a four-day trip. Charlie went to visit his family in Texas. When everyone returned, the branding would begin and shortly after, the harvest. This was a welcomed break.

Marc would stay on the ranch with Mrs. Courtley, who was still attending her class each morning. He would see that everything remained status quo. The cattle had been driven together, closer, and they were checked every day and being fed bales of hay to keep them from wandering off again into the hills. Otherwise he did odd jobs that were necessary, and worked on the machinery, and was in the barn and near the house while Mrs. Courtley was home. Bonnie Lass tagged after Marc, not letting him out of sight.

Mrs. Courtley insisted that Marc have his evening meal with her. He enjoyed this immensely, for Mrs. Courtley was easy to talk with, and although the meals were simple, they were delicious. The first evening, they talked of his family, his future schooling — only light things — and he very carefully avoided any subject concerning Carrie or her brother.

Pictures were abundantly displayed in the front room, the same as in Winger's house, and in one corner there were shelves of the trophies and ribbons that Allen had won. Marc knew instinctively that he would have liked Allen Courtley V.

The second evening, it was Mrs. Courtley who brought up the subject of Carrie's brother, and Marc saw that she did it purposely.

Mrs. Courtley liked Marc. She understood her daughter's intense struggle and how Marc affected her. The struggle was Carrie's alone, but the path could be made smoother with understanding. On the other side, she didn't want to see Marc hurt. He was a sensitive, caring person, and Carrie was lashing out, using Marc as the target. It wasn't fair to Marc.

Mrs. Courtley settled on the sofa while Marc sat opposite in one of the big, overstuffed easy chairs.

"That's my husband's favorite chair," Mrs. Courtley said casually.

Marc laughed. "I can see why."

"Carrie was not an only child. We also had a son, you know," Mrs. Courtley began, and touched one of the pictures on the end table. "This is our son."

Embarrassment surfaced before Marc could check it.

"Oh, Marc, it's all right. We speak of Allen freely, but I do believe that Carrie has some anger toward you. Am I right?" she questioned.

Marc protested, "Oh, no explanation is necessary. I just take things as they are."

"Marc, you're more than a ranch hand. You are helping Carrie in a very special way, whether you know it or not, and it is far more than training a horse," Mrs. Courtley said in total honesty. But she saw that he was still puzzled, not knowing how to react or what to say. Softly she added, "I don't mean to embarrass you. Let me tell you about Allen. I think that will help you understand a few things more clearly."

So she talked of her son, lovingly, without morbid sadness. She told how Carrie, being a more introspective person, had followed each daring stunt with extreme concern, but also with complete admiration. Everything Allen attempted, he did well: school, sports, riding, just everything. He was Carrie's hero. To see him trampled lifeless before her eyes was something almost insurmountable for her to bear.

Being intuitive, Marc understood how he affected Carrie. "And I am an intrusion, trying

105

to take his place, jarring memories best forgotten."

Mrs. Courtley smiled. That was the only answer Marc needed to know that he had been right. He began to have another view of Carrie. He thought of her at the cemetery. It made more sense now.

"But you know, Marc," Mrs. Courtley went on, "beyond the hostility, which you can understand, you are forcing Carrie to push aside this unhealthy attachment to her brother. She has to assume her own identity, which is happening through her riding. She certainly can't cling to her brother, and I would say that you are a very special person to have spotted the trouble without knowing the facts or reason."

Marc was embarrassed again. "Well, it is only because I know horses so well. My grandfather gave me that special gift with animals. I must admit I didn't know why Carrie reacted as she did to everything I said or did. It completely baffled me."

"You are very much like Allen," Mrs. Courtley confided. "I see it. So does Carrie, and it frightens her. It threatens her image of Allen and she doesn't know how to fit you anywhere. So, she keeps you, in her eyes at least, as strictly summer help."

Marc smiled. There was no answer to that.

They were both quiet, thoughtful. It was comfortable.

"Thanks for telling me," Marc said finally. "It helps."

"I thought so. We are a quiet family, letting each other work things out on their own. Carrie would never mean to hurt you. That, I want you to fully understand," Mrs. Courtley emphasized.

Again, Marc smiled. An open, friendly smile that clearly said he understood.

"Now I had better get back to my books. It's good to be on the student side for a while. It makes you remember how it feels. Being a teacher, you tend to forget," Mrs. Courtley said, laughing.

With this they both arose and said good night.

Marc strolled slowly through the tall cedars and past the garage. It was strange not to see lights in Winger's house and stranger still to have a whole house to himself.

He thought a lot about Carrie. She was different from anyone he had ever known. Suddenly her image captured him. The thick red hair flowing free about her, the deep blue of her eyes, which reflected what was going on inside. A tenderness engulfed him, the same as so many times before when he was near her.

He knew fully well that the feelings he had for Carrie were not ones that a brother would have toward a sister. He had too many sisters and knew the difference. Nor were they the simple, concerned feelings a trainer-coach would have toward a student. No, the feelings were far more. It fringed on love. At least he thought so, but then, how would he know? He had never felt this way about a girl. What is the difference between like or love, or mere infatuation? Where is the dividing line? Maybe it was the special caring that made the difference and that he did like Carrie. That was puzzling after the way she had treated him.

Marc leaned against the corral fence and sighed. Low clouds crossed the moon. A breeze to which he had paid no attention earlier drew his notice. It blew the scent of rain — strong, refreshing, and welcomed. Perhaps the prediction would come true.

He started again for the adobe house, a bit faster this time. What did his feelings matter? Carrie saw him only as a trainer, summer help; those things and a threat to the memory of replacing her brother. Well, a little more than a month and he'd be gone, so why stir up emotions that would come to nothing but hurt. He did understand her frame of reference now, and if he helped her achieve her goals and a clearer sense of herself, he'd be satisfied.

NINE

ON a Saturday, everyone returned.

Carrie, ecstatic, ran to tell her mother that she had received a second, third, and a fifth. A real improvement.

"That is wonderful!" her mother cried, letting Carrie dance her around the kitchen.

"I did it! I did it!" Carrie sang over and over again. "And people said that I rode almost as well as Allen!"

Her mother stopped her in middance. "How well did you ride as Caroline Courtley?"

Carrie stared into her mother's serious eyes. The point was made and the message received. Carrie grimaced, then she answered in a small voice, "I rode super as Caroline Courtley, Mom."

"Good," her mother replied, and gave her daughter a quick hug. "Have you shared this good news with Marc?"

"Later, Mom. Right now I've got to help get Morning Star into the pasture. Character is still there, I see," and she ran off without any further reference to Marc.

It was late afternoon. Would Winger be

home? Their car was there, and Cleo would be there for sure. Maybe her father had already told them. She hoped not. She wanted to share the good news herself.

Morning Star was eager to pasture after the long confinement in the horse trailer. She ran around and around, shaking her head, stopping to turn sharply and run in the opposite direction. The chestnut joined her in the frolic. Morning Star's white coat was a startling contrast to the deep red of the chestnut.

"You run!" Carrie hollered. "You deserve it!" She watched a few minutes longer, then scooted up the hill toward Winger's house, her hair flying out behind her.

Just as she was running up the stone steps leading to the back porch, she saw Marc. He was driving the jeep toward the barn. Instinctively, Carrie knew that he had seen her, and she should have stopped and called him, telling him the good news. But she didn't. Instead, she flew through the door onto the screened porch and into the house without a knock.

"Cleo! Winger!" she yelled.

Cleo was in the kitchen, and, as Carrie whizzed through the door she turned exclaiming, "Here she is! Here she is!"

"You've heard already!" Carrie said, pretending to pout.

Cleo laughed. "Not really. Your dad just said that you had good news to share. So share away! Are you hungry?"

"How can you think of food? I feel so great! Where is Winger?" Carrie whirled into the front room after Cleo pointed.

"Well, Kitten, come here and tell me," Winger urged, his face crinkled into a complete smile. He was watching a baseball game on television. Cleo, who had followed right on Carrie's heels, settled on the arm of the easy chair while Carrie turned the volume down.

Then she shot around, yelling, "Hear ye! Hear ye! you are looking upon a person who placed . . . second! Third! And fifth!"

"Hurray!" Cleo shouted, and jumped up applauding.

"That is wonderful, Carrie," Winger said. "I always knew you could do it. Yes, sir, that's our Carrie. And, I'd say that Marc Bear is a better teacher than I am. Have you told him?"

Carrie looked directly at Winger. "No. You can tell him when he comes to eat supper," she announced, and with heated feeling, she added, "If you hadn't been busy you would still be training with me, and I would have done just as well!"

Cleo and Winger, responding to the edge in her voice, cast a hurried signal with their eyes and dropped the subject. Then there was an exciting play in the baseball game and Winger turned the volume up with his remote control. Cleo motioned Carrie back into the kitchen.

"Baseball! It does something to a man's brain! Makes them little boys again, that's what.

But now," Cleo begged with sincere zest, "tell me about the horse show . . . every little detail. I'm going to start supper while you talk. Too late for a roast so I thought meat loaf would do as well. They'll like it just as well, don't you think? I'm trying a new recipe."

Carrie sat at the kitchen table, drumming her fingers. "Cleo!" She laughed. "So do you want to hear this or not?!"

Grinning, Cleo put her fingers to her lips so Carrie could begin her four-day saga. All the while, Cleo worked at the preparations for supper, nodding in approval. She must have just washed her short hair, for it was a bit frizzy, bobbing with every nod. Carrie thought it was funny, so she made the story a bit more exaggerated, giving Cleo more to nod about.

At the end of it all, Cleo clapped her hands, exclaiming, "That is wonderful!"

"Now I've got to run. If Mom calls, tell her I'm on my way," Carrie said, getting up from the table, and with a wave she was out the back door.

At the back steps, Carrie paused to scan the area around the barn and corral. No one in sight. It was Marc she didn't want to see right now. They would work together again on Monday, and by that time he would have heard about her placings in the show. If she saw him now, well, the conversation would be stiff and formal, void of the enthusiasm that she felt. But he should be the one to hear the good news first.

But that is the way it was since they had agreed to avoid each other.

It was cloudy again with a chill in the air, and during the night it rained. Thunder growled across the sky like the far-off rumbles of Rip Van Winkle's tenpin game, but Sunday morning found the sky blown clear. About midmorning the phone rang through the quiet house.

Carrie was in the kitchen cleaning up after a late breakfast. "Maybe it's Debbie," Carrie hoped out loud. "She didn't go to this last show. I sure want to tell her my news and I can't seem to get her at home. Maybe John told her."

Her father reached the extension in the office first. It was not Debbie. It was Winger. She could tell by the way her dad talked, and he spoke so loudly Carrie could hear him clearly in the kitchen.

"Are you sure?" her father demanded. "I thought we had put a stop to that! I'll be right over." And with that, he slammed down the receiver.

Anger never surfaced easily with Allen Courtley IV, and if it did, it was usually quietly expressed. To see it burst forth like this meant something was very wrong.

Mrs. Courtley was coming down the stairs when she heard her husband's angry voice. "What is it, Allen?" she asked anxiously, walking quickly to the office.

He stood at his desk in thought, his mouth shut in a tight line.

"Allen?" she repeated.

"Winger rode out early this morning to check the cattle to find many of them had been driven back into the hills again."

"The storm?" she interjected quickly.

He shook his head. "No. That kind of storm would never scatter cattle like that. The thunder was deep and rolling. It's the sharp electrical cracking kind that spooks animals. You know that."

She nodded. She knew that, but it was a straw to grasp at. Something had frightened the animals. Mrs. Courtley stood waiting for her husband to explain further, and Carrie came from the kitchen to listen also.

"It's those punks who come out of nowhere to chase animals for fun. With jeeps, of course. Remember when we had this some years back? We got rid of them then, and I thought it was the end of that nonsense. But here it is again, and the damage is done. We'll have to round up the scattered cattle again. I just hope that's all the damage they did. Well, that changes our plans for branding on Tuesday."

The outward anger was checked, and Allen Courtley was again his usual calm self. What he felt inside was another story, but he was not a man who liked to lose control. He hurried over to Winger's house with Carrie and Bonnie Lass right on his heels. To keep up with his long, quick strides, Carrie had to almost run. Her father was upset and she didn't ask any questions, not when he was like this. This was serious. Any cattle loss to a rancher was a direct attack on his bank account, his investment, his livelihood. It was never taken lightly. The weather was out of a rancher's control, but his cattle . . . well, that he could watch and protect.

When they entered Winger's house the frustration was being loudly vented. Winger was plain mad. Both Marc and Charlie stood in the kitchen near the windows, listening, waiting to be of some help, whatever it might be. They had never seen Winger like this but Carrie had, and she remained next to her father, quiet as a mouse. Carrie knew just how riled Winger could get over something like this.

"They've headed back into the hills, Allen. The tracks are still visible. The rain didn't wipe them out completely. Maybe they're camping back there. Who knows?" He talked loudly, almost to the point of shouting, and paced about the kitchen pounding his fist on an open palm, as if he were punching whoever had done this right on the nose. "I suppose they are now back there disturbing those mustangs. That's their idea of sport. Some sport! Chasing horses until they are exhausted!" he jeered.

Cleo posted herself at the stove, shaking her head with distress written all over her face. She was more worried about Winger than the cattle. She hated to see her husband in this state, yet she said nothing. It would do no good.

"What's to be done here, other than round up those cattle again?" Winger asked Mr. Courtley. He stopped his pacing and stood beside his friend and boss. Having worked together for years, they understood each other very well and just about knew what the other would do.

Mr. Courtley responded in a steady, clear manner. "First, call Finney, and tell him to take his branding crew to another ranch on Tuesday. We won't be ready. That's clear. Next, let's get our camping gear together and root out whoever is back there in those hills before more damage is done."

Winger nodded vigorously in agreement. "The sooner, the better. Want to go back far enough to check on those mustangs?"

"They just may be clear back there. We'll have their jeep tracks to tell us that," Mr. Courtley said.

Carrie drew a quick breath. The mustangs! The black mare! She was suddenly upset at the thought of someone harrassing the wild horses. She had thought of them, in a sense, as belonging to her brother. He was the one who used to go back into hills for days at a time to watch them. Someone was tampering with the memory of her brother again. Her hand flew to her throat in alarm.

All this time, Marc had been listening, his eyes cast downward, as if pondering the situation, but he caught Carrie's panicky movement immediately. A week ago he would not have understood. Alarm mirrored in her eyes. They widened, as if she were actually seeing the mustangs.

Marc felt a caring warmth arise. He continued

to watch her until she felt his extended gaze and was drawn to look back in return. Their eyes met, and in that instant, Carrie read something she had not seen before. He knows, she thought. He knows about Allen and the mustang. He knows why I resent him. It was as if he could see straight through her. Her mother! It must have been her mother who told him.

Her composure crumbled further. He knows that I placed high at the horse show and didn't bother to tell him. She felt her face glow and her whole body was hot from embarrassment. She turned to listen to her father, but she was only too conscious of Marc's stare. Did it please him to see her so rattled? she thought angrily. But when she peered again in his direction, he was talking with Charlie in a low voice and not looking at her at all.

Cleo had already gotten a box and was packing food after telephoning Mrs. Courtley first. It was then that Carrie decided that she was going back into the hills with them. Hastily she fled to the door, and as she left the kitchen she heard her father say that he would call Sheriff Coolsey, in case he had to make a citizen's arrest.

Poor Bonnie Lass didn't know what all the running back and forth was about, but she stuck close to Carrie. As Carrie ran, her thoughts tumbled about, confused. She didn't understand herself! Up to this point, going into the hills had been totally repulsive. Sometimes the very thought of that black mare had made her sick to her stomach. She hated that horse! She hated it but she felt compelled to go back into the hills with her father. Yes, compelled was the feeling. Why? Why would she even wish to see the horse that had brought her such pain and misery?

She found her mother in the kitchen, packing, just as Cleo was. Camping gear was already sitting by the door. As Carrie burst through the door, Sarah Courtley stopped, startled, and when Carrie yelled, "I'm going, too!" shock spread across her face.

Her mother immediately dropped what she was doing to follow Carrie as she sped up the stairs and into her bedroom.

"Carrie!" her mother cried. "What are you talking about?" She remained calm, but the deep, sudden concern was clearly evident in her voice. "It's dangerous to go back into the hills, especially if those men are marauding back there. What does your father say?"

Mrs. Courtley stood by the closet door, for that is where Carrie had disappeared to. "I didn't ask Daddy," came the muffled answer. Out of the closet she pulled out her heavy riding boots, a jacket, some sweaters, and finally, her sleeping bag. Everything landed in a heap on the floor. When she emerged from the closet, she headed for her dresser and pulled open the top drawer. "Mother, my heavy socks. Where are they?"

But her mother wasn't interested in socks. "Carrie, I don't understand this at all. You have never wanted to go into the hills, not even with your father. Ever since Allen . . ." She didn't finish. She followed her daughter to the dresser, waiting for some kind of explanation.

"Can't I change my mind, Mom?" Carrie asked without stopping her frantic search. "Socks. Socks, where are you?" She found them in the second drawer.

"Those men could have guns, Carrie. If they are crazy enough to chase harmless animals, who knows what they are capable of?" her mother admonished.

Carrie realized her mother was very concerned and she stopped, saying, "Honest, I won't get hurt. Mom, I can't explain it, but I want to go. I haven't felt like this before, and I wouldn't have gone before, but today, for some reason, it's different." She looked at her mother and pleaded, "Please ask Dad. It's important."

Looking into her daughter's serious, begging eyes Mrs. Courtley could see that this was more than a whim. To Carrie, this was important. It was difficult to believe, knowing how she would have reacted to going into the hills just a month ago, or even to a suggestion of going into the hills.

"All right, honey, I'll talk with your father," her mother conceded.

"Oh, thanks, Mom," Carrie said, giving her mother a quick squeeze. "Now I've got to get ready, so I won't be considered a hindrance."

That closed the argument. Reluctantly Sarah Courtley walked from the room, a slight frown revealing her disapproval. She was not fully con-

vinced this was the right thing for Carrie. Yet . . .
this may well be a milestone for her daughter. A
sign of growth, one that was necessary. Was it
she who was afraid? Afraid to let go, afraid
something might happen to Carrie as it had to
Allen?

She heard the screen door squeak, and she
knew that her husband had come for the gear
and food. She hurried down the stairs.

Within an hour they were ready to go. She was
sitting astride Character next to the jeep, waiting for last-minute things to be checked. Her
mother, standing near Mr. Courtley, still wore a
slightly worried look. Carrie smiled at her.

"Where is Bee Line?" she asked her father.
She knew they were taking an extra horse and
had expected to lead it as she rode.

"Marc is getting him. He'll have the horse
ready and waiting at the back pasture," her father answered.

Winger arrived, out of breath, from his house.
"Let's get started," he fretted. They were all
anxious; Winger showed it outwardly. This was
not a pleasant trek into the hills. Usually they
went back there to hunt or fish, but who knew
what this trip would bring!

Already behind the wheel, Mr. Courtley
started the engine. Winger swung in beside him.
"Let's go," Mr. Courtley said. "I want to be in
those hills before dark!" He then turned to his
wife and said softly, "Everything will be fine,
mother."

With that, the jeep pulled away from the

garage slowly, and up past Winger's house where Cleo waved from the front window. Morning Star trotted along the pasture fence whinnying and tossing her head as if in protest. What was Carrie doing on another horse leaving her behind in the pasture? Carrie galloped over to the fence to comfort her with a pat.

"Now, now girl. I'll be back to ride you. But you're for show, not for the hills. You understand?" Carrie said soothingly. She rubbed her between her ears. "Got to go now!" And Carrie set out fast after the jeep.

When they reached the back pasture, there was Marc waiting with Bee Line. The horse was saddled and ready to go. Marc leaned casually against the gate with a long piece of grass drooping from his mouth, which he threw to ground as the jeep approached. Carrie drew in behind the jeep, expecting to take the reins, so she could lead Bee Line, when she heard her father say, "Now, son, we'll go fairly slow so as not to tire the horses, but we will keep a steady pace. You won't have any trouble." Then her father started off again.

In disbelief, Carrie watched as Marc swung his agile body smoothly into the saddle, then, giving Carrie a small salute, he trotted after the jeep. Stunned, Carrie sat there. All of her expectations of the exciting adventure crumbled. This had seemed a private trip to Carrie, a link somehow between she and Allen. How many times had her brother traveled this very path just as they were doing now? In disgust, she urged Character forward. To turn back now would only reveal her pride and selfishness. Her father would question her actions, and then her motives, plus it would hurt Marc. That she knew, and she had done enough of that already! A dull sensation in the pit of her stomach signaled that she didn't like herself very much right now.

Her father had stopped the jeep up ahead, and waved her on, calling, "Caroline, keep up with us!"

She was trailing behind. "Caroline!" That was saved only for the times her father was upset or irritated; or on the other side of the coin, when particularly gentle. She spurred the horse to a gallop, and when she caught up she apologized. "Sorry, Dad."

A scowl was her answer. "Marc, see that she stays with you." Without another word, he drove on.

That stung! Treated like a child not able to keep pace! Marc waited. Her distress was obvious, but he remained silent. She would have thought he would be pleased to see her slightly humiliated and put in his care. A taste of the hurt she had aimed at him, intentionally or unintentionally, but no hint of laughter reflected on his face. Only kindness rested in those thick-lashed eyes.

It threw Carrie. She felt that she had been hit. Not with the return of resentment that she so rightly deserved, but with understanding. She was confused. She had decided to shut him out, but he continued to treat her with kindness.

Maybe it wasn't kindness, but pity. She would hate that even more. Whatever it was, as she sat there looking into his eyes, she was suddenly drawn to Marc Bear, irresistibly drawn, with an impact that made her want to suddenly reach out to him. It was frightening; Marc was gentle and kind to her, but he sat there as aloof and distant as ever. She clicked Character into a run and Marc followed.

TEN

THEY stopped first at the herd of milling cattle. This was not the entire herd but the ones that would need the branding of the Courtley ranch. There were few fences, especially back in the hills. When it came time for branding or selling, there was a general round-up of the animals. These animals had not been brought into a closely fenced area, but near the spot where the branding would take place. They were kept content, and together, by the bales of hay brought to them daily.

As Mr. Courtley pulled to a stop on a rise above the cattle, he could see that about a third of them had been badly scattered. Thinking that the jeep may panic them after their recent chase, it was decided that Marc would ride down and around to see if there were tracks more recent than the ones Winger had seen. The cattle would not scatter with a horse among them.

That day's bales of hay had been dumped and spread earlier that morning, so the animals were more interested in them than they were in Marc. He rode, skirting the herd, looking to see whether the men had driven back the way they had come.

Carrie stayed on Character near the jeep. Her father and Winger had walked off some distance to examine the road ahead. It seemed that the men had headed for the back hills.

Still feeling the sting of resentment that Marc had been included in the investigation, Carrie sat following Marc's every move as he wound himself among the cattle and around the edges of the herd. Easy. Relaxed. Watching him, she wondered what he, knowing about her brother, thought of her.

Briefly, she tried to put herself in his place. How would he see her? The very thought made her sigh. Surely he didn't like her! How could he? Every time he came near, she responded like a prickly porcupine, bristling with pointed, sharp words. No, he could not possibly like her. Sitting there quietly in the warmth of the sun, feeling secure knowing her father and Winger were close by, she had to admit to herself that she was glad Marc was with them. She could not deny that any more than she could deny that she liked Marc Bear. There was nothing not to like. The resentment lay in having to admit it.

Why had her mother told him about Allen? Carrie smiled. Her mother would have a reason. It was not just idle talk, and she had to remember, that she alone had the hostility toward Marc. Everyone else held him in high regard. She sighed again. If only her father had hired an older man, another one like Charlie, none of this would be happening.

In about twenty minutes, Marc spurred Bee Line back toward the jeep, and Carrie saw that her father and Winger, too, were walking in the same direction. The pace was determined, their faces serious, and neither spoke while they walked. They reached the jeep before Marc and climbed in immediately, waiting to hear what news he would bring from below, if any.

"Well, son, what did you find?" came her father's direct question as Marc reined in beside the jeep.

"They haven't been back. There were no tracks or scattered cattle Friday morning, I'm sure of that. They must have come in Friday afternoon or sometime Saturday. I didn't come out on Saturday, and I now I see I should have," Marc said, feeling he had let Mr. Courtley down.

"That's nonsense, Marc. It isn't your fault. How could you have predicted a thing like this," Mr. Courtley reassured him.

"Well, the tracks are the ones they made when they came in," Marc restated.

"It's very plain that they've headed back, and if they have left, it is by a very different route. We need to find that out," Mr. Courtley said, his voice edged with dislike for the whole business.

All this time, Carrie had been scanning Marc's face as he talked with her father. It was plain that he was disturbed by this turn of events, and for not coming Saturday to check the cattle. Winger sat silent, just waiting to be on the way.

Carrie had not bothered to braid her hair as she usually did when she rode, and although she was wearing her western hat, a sudden gust of wind whipped her hair, blowing it across her face. She turned her head downward as if to avoid getting the hair in her eyes, and as she did so, something caught her eye out over the hills. It gave her shivers. Vultures!

The jeep was parked so that the circling birds were out of her father's view, and they had been so busy searching the ground for tracks, the sky had been neglected.

"Dad, look!" Carrie exclaimed, and pointed to soaring vultures, their wings spread in almost motionless flight above the brushy hills.

They all swung their heads in the direction, and, of course, they all knew what that meant. Dead animals.

Winger reacted first. "Well, it looks like they may have managed to drive some of them to their death," he angrily affirmed. "Let's hope it's only wild animals."

Mr. Courtley jerked them back. "Let's be on our way. Charlie will come out later today to check things again." It was plain he was restless. All of you keep those tracks in sight and see if I'm not right . . . that they lead back into the hills."

Winger glanced at his watch, then up at Carrie. "Ready? Can you keep up, Kitten?" A twinkle sparked his gray eyes, although no smile was even suggested on his face. Typical of him.

"Winger!" she shot back, her eyes wide. She had often been the target of his quiet teasing. It didn't matter; in fact, she rather enjoyed it. But today? Please not now!

Her father suppressed a smile, the corners of

his mouth twitching. He started the engine and slowly pulled away. Marc didn't look at her but took out after the jeep.

For three hours the jeep wound its way back into the wild, rugged country. The road was a narrow, two-rutted ribbon that bent and twisted with the uneven design of the hills. The jeep bounced and roared, but a steady pace was kept. Both Carrie and Marc stayed a fair distance behind the jeep to avoid the exhaust and dirt that flew out in its trail.

As Carrie rode beside Marc, each of them following one of the ruts, she thought of many things. Her mother, for one. She hoped that her mother was not sitting at home worrying. Maybe she would stay with Cleo tonight. Cleo would like that; she hated to have Winger gone. But then Carrie wondered why she had never really sat down with her mother and talked this whole thing out . . . about Marc. Her mother was such a good listener, an understanding listener. Even the kids at school sought her out to talk to as a sounding board. Why hadn't she — her own daughter? The only person she had truly confided in was Debbie. Well, for one thing, Debbie wouldn't scold. That was it. Underneath it all, Carrie knew she was ashamed of her own rudeness, selfishness, and whatever else, and if she had confided in her mother, it would be made apparent; but, if her mother didn't know, well . . . only Marc would know. Marc never mentioned it to anyone, and she could hide behind that as well.

That was rotten . . . plain rotten. Marc had done nothing to warrant her rudeness and resentment, except to be on the ranch. He had asked so little, not even to be a friend, but to share a common interest: horses. And Marc could have been a friend, a good one, just as her brother had been to her. Pangs of regret crept in, mingling with the guilt. She realized how unfair she had been to him, and to herself.

She drank in the beautiful countryside. Tall mountain pines covered the slopes. It was peaceful, orderly, like a tonic at least for now, until they discovered who or what was marauding farther back. The peace could well be gone. Carrie drew a deep breath. Maybe this is why her brother had packed back into the loneliness of the forest. It wasn't lonely at all . . . not in the sad sense. The pettiness of everyday life faded completely in the serenity of nature's grandeur. What would rudeness mean to a forest? One could be rude all day and still the trees would stand in silent defiance: growing, being, sheltering, swaying; and would they care? The rudeness would leave no mark.

Glancing sideways at Marc, she wondered what he was thinking. Not of her, certainly. And that made her feel sorry; yes, actually and suddenly sorry. Debbie had been right . . . she *did* like Marc Bear. It had taken another person to see what she did not. Marc could never take Allen's place as a brother, and peering at him now, she would not want him as a brother. How dumb everything was! It had never occurred to her to think of any boy she knew as anything other than a friend. Like? Love? No, never. It had to fall on her like a ton of bricks, or was it more like running into a brick wall; either way, it took this long for the bricks to fall.

The jeep braked to a stop, pulling off the road to rest under a huge pine. As Carrie and Marc caught up, they saw why. There, not too far down a fairly steep incline, was a rushing mountain stream. Narrow, bubbling, and truly babbling, with ferns bowing above it in rhythm to the breeze that furrowed through the trees.

"The horses will need a drink and a rest," Mr. Courtley said. He climbed out of the jeep and stretched his legs, as did Winger. Then he took a thermos out of the box her mother had packed, and he poured himself a cup of coffee. Winger took a cup also, but Marc declined.

After tying Bee Line to a tree, Marc set out with her father and Winger to examine the road up ahead. Carrie was left to water her horse alone. She dismounted and led Character down the incline to the stream. Oh, she hated disturbing the ferns, trampling them. They grew so close, their large sprawling leaves touching, one plant to another, and another . . . spreading a waving sea of green among the trees. But they were trampled where she and Character walked, cutting a path through the thick green covering. While the horse drank, Carrie knelt beside the icy water to wash her hands and face. It was wonderful. It was so cold, it tingled to the tip of her toes.

She hoped that Marc would water his horse at the same time, for she had promised herself she would be friendlier. The guilt was really beginning to surface and she was tripping over it at every turn. But Marc did not come near her. Again, true to his word, he let her alone, even now on the trail with her father and Winger. What began to worry Carrie was that her father would notice and, of course, he finally did.

Character finished his long drink, and Carrie slowly climbed back up the steep slope leading the horse. The men had just returned. Winger helped himself to another cup of coffee, talking all the while to her dad. Marc had already untied Bee Line and was starting down the slope. He smiled at Carrie but said nothing.

Her dad consulted his watch. "Another two hours and we'll be at the ridge. Get there about five, I'd say, which will leave enough daylight to scout about some. Are we about ready?" He looked to see where Marc was at the moment.

"Are there still tracks on the road, Dad?" Carrie asked, coming close to her father.

"Yup, there are," he answered.

Winger tossed out what little coffee there was in the bottom of the cup and put it back into the box. "Want to ride in the jeep, Kitten?" he asked. There was no teasing this time, only concern.

Carrie shook her head. "No, I'm fine."

Then her father asked the question she had been dreading. "Are you and Marc at odds with each other?"

Carrie stiffened and answered too quickly, "No, why?"

The hurried tone made her father look at her closely, his eyes seeking hers while Carrie avoided his intense gaze by fussing with Character and patting him on the nose and adjusting the bridle.

"Why are you so cool to each other? You don't even talk. You should be friends; he has been on the ranch long enough, and you've trained together," her father said quietly.

She had no answer, and she shot Winger a "help" look from beneath the wide brim of her western hat.

He raised his eyebrows, widening his eyes, but remained silent.

Her father, seeing the exchange of glances and not getting an answer, became more suspicious. "Has Marc been out of place with you and you didn't tell me?!" There was a quiet, steellike demand in his voice. He wanted an answer.

Carrie was horrified. "Oh, Daddy, never!" Even Winger drew back, catching his breath.

"Then what?" You aren't natural with each other, not even friendly," Mr. Courtley stated flatly.

Out of the corner of her eye she saw Marc coming back up the incline. Panic gripped her. She could not meet her father's gaze or answer his question. There was no simple answer. She knew her father's demands when it came to the help on the ranch. They were to be treated kindly, and that is all her father could see right now . . . the cool unkindness.

Winger stepped in quietly. "It's not that, Allen. I think Carrie here is having some growing pains. That's all, and she is trying to sort a few things out."

"Daddy, please!" Carrie pleaded in a whisper. "I'll explain later." Tears sprang involuntarily. Oh, she didn't want Marc to hear this conversation.

Mr. Courtley's tone changed as she finally met his probing gaze, and on seeing the tears, he knew Carrie was having a struggle of some kind. "All right," he conceded. He then turned to get in the jeep while Winger helped her into the saddle.

Leaning forward, she whispered, "Thanks, Winger — for that and for not telling Dad how awful I've been to Marc."

"First love is not easy," Winger whispered, and gave her a gentle pat for reassurance. Then he, too, climbed back into the jeep.

Carrie couldn't believe her ears. Winger knew! He knew all the time, just like Debbie! But then, Winger had been with her more because of training with her. He had time to see what was really troubling her while her father didn't.

Marc had now reached the road and remounted. As he brought his horse in beside Carrie's, a questioning flicker appeared briefly in his eyes, but when Mr. Courtley called, "Everyone ready?" he simply smiled at Carrie. The tears that were still moist at the corners of her eyes had puzzled him, but when Mr. Courtley pulled ahead with the jeep, they followed.

The tire tracks appeared and disappeared on

the rutted road depending upon whether there was sand, gravel, or rock, but they continued to lead farther back. It was someone who definitely knew the road was there. This land was strictly private and posted but once someone had wound their way to find the land almost untouched, they didn't forget it, nor would they tell anyone else. Whether the land was posted or not did not mean much to some people.

Pushing farther and farther into the hills, Carrie began to wonder about the mustangs. Would they be there, and would they see them? A tingle of fear and anticipation went through her. Somehow, right now, she didn't mind having Marc along; in fact, she liked it. What was wrong with her? A few hours ago, she had bucked like a wild horse at the thought of his being a part of his trek. It must be the countryside, the clear mountain air, the prayerful solitude of the surrounding peaks, the towering pines. It stilled her troubled thoughts and settled them into perspective. Could it be possible that some months ago she thought of Marc as a brash smart aleck who stared at girls, a deliberate intruder nosing where he was not wanted, and, in her mind, usurping her brother's place in her heart and her father's?

She laughed inwardly. None of it was true. It had been her own concept of it all the time. Poor Marc. She was glad that her mother had talked to him, and had not mentioned it to her father. Growing pains, Winger had said. That was putting it mildly, and she felt a surge of gratitude for her family, and that included Winger and Cleo.

It had never been Marc that she had hated, but herself, fighting her own grief and anger. Peering at Marc now, riding so easily beside her, her hatred for him melted like the winter snow on a warm spring day. Her brother, so free and full of life when he was here, would have liked Marc at once. Was it too late? What could she do? There was Marc, so close, that if they reached out they could touch hands, but oh, he was so far. She had chased his warm generous nature into that cool aloofness, and now who would know what or how he felt!

The two hours passed quickly, and they reached the ridge overlooking the valley before five o'clock. This was the first time Carrie had ever been this far back, but her father and Winger had camped here often, as had her brother. Not far from the small clearing was a mountain stream, somewhat wider than the one they had stopped at earlier. Opposite the stream at the edge of the ridge was an opening in the trees that looked like a huge window, and from there the whole sweep of the valley was in view. A beautiful, green meadow stretched before their eyes.

Carrie, so smitten with it all, was pulled back to reality by her father. Camp had to be set up. That meant they had to get busy before dusk settled in. Hurry was the word. Winger and Marc set out at once to see what they could find down in the valley. The jeep could be heard grinding its way down the steep, twisted hillside trail long after it had disappeared from sight.

A pup tent had been brought for Carrie, and although she had protested, her mother had won. Her father now set it up. It didn't take long. Carrie tackled the folding camp table. On this was set a small kerosene camp stove. After a few pumps of the tank handle and match, there was a fire for a pot of coffee.

"That will bring them out of the valley in a hurry," Carrie laughed as she put the large enamelware coffee pot on the burner. "The aroma of coffee!"

There was enough food that they didn't really have to cook, and the only other thing they did was to spread pine boughs and needles where they would place the sleeping bags. The men would sleep in the open.

Carrie took the one box out of the jeep and set it on the folding table. It was Cleo's box of food, and as Carrie began to dig through it, she laughed. "You are not going to believe this, Dad. You are not going to believe it! We could stay here a week and never run out of food."

"Well, hunger won't be the problem, will it?" her father replied. "Your mother packed food, too."

"I know! I know!" Carrie said. "Tonight we had better eat the fried chicken. Everything else is canned.

"How about a fire?" her father asked, and before she answered he had already begun to stack firewood in a circle of stones that had been placed in the center of the clearing on some previous camping trip. There were also logs alongside, to be used for sitting. Certainly no one had been in this clearing to disturb anything; only some persistent weeds had intruded, and those were quickly pulled.

Once the fire began to burn steadily, Mr. Courtley rummaged in Cleo's box of food, coming up with several pieces of chicken.

"Dad!" Carrie asked, "Aren't you going to wait for the others?"

"Nope!" was the calm reply. He came and sat next to his daughter on the log next to the fire. "This fire will make you feel mighty good. You did bring heavy clothes with you, didn't you?"

"I did," she answered, then becoming more serious, she started, "Dad?"

"Hmmm?" He had a mouthful of chicken.

"Dad? Do you like Marc Bear?" she asked softly.

Her father swallowed, then turned to look at her. "That's a strange question." And he continued to look at her as if not sure how to answer. The horses, tethered near the stream where they could drink, snickered and nibbled the hay brought for them, and other than the singing of the stream, it was quiet.

"Is there any reason I shouldn't like Marc Bear, or better still, is there any reason that you don't like him?" her father countered.

"That is what I want to talk to you about," Carrie said. "I promised you I would." Yes, she had promised, and she had better do it before

Marc returned, otherwise her father would again give her the third degree, because things between she and Marc had not changed. The ice was still there. "Mother hasn't said anything to you, I see."

Her father frowned. "What is this, Carrie? What is wrong with Marc? And why should your mother say anything to me?" His voice was stern.

"Oh, Daddy," Carrie groaned. "It isn't Marc . . . it's me. It's me!" Then she told her father everything, even how nasty she had been to Marc, and she finished up by saying, "And to make matters worse, I like Marc. I mean that I *like* him. You know how I mean, Daddy."

"Yes, I know," he answered. He shook his head. "I had no idea you were having this struggle."

"Well, I was ashamed because everyone else liked him, and I knew you would come down hard on me," Carrie fully admitted.

"Yes, you're right," was his frank answer. "And Marc is like Allen in many ways. I guess that's why it's so easy for me to call him son. But he would never take Allen's place. How could you even imagine that?"

"When you're upset, Daddy, you can imagine anything," Carrie confided.

They were both still, watching the fire. It had begun to snap and pop in earnest.

"You know, honey, you were so young to see that happen to Allen. It would be difficult for anyone, at any age, but I marvel that it hasn't bothered you more. You're sturdy stuff, Carrie.

We, being older, had more practice at handling tragedy; at least, I like to think so. Grief is never easy. I see that you handled it in a way right for you at your time of experience. What else could you do? We let Allen go. It is always necessary when someone dies. It doesn't mean you love them less. But you see, you clung to Allen, making him a hero image, even more so, because of your riding. That isn't loving your brother, Carrie because, as you see, it was harming you. It would keep you from liking, or even loving, someone as fine as Marc Bear."

He was right, and now Carrie knew it. He could say it without her fighting back and refusing to see the truth. "But what can I do, Daddy? I've hurt Marc, to the point that he avoids me."

Far off they could hear the jeep winding its way back up the rugged road. Winger and Marc would be in the clearing before dark.

"Just be yourself, Caroline. You are a lovely person and I can say that with honesty, and somehow I think that Marc knows that, too. Love your brother but in the proper context and perspective. It isn't easy. And, I think, too, a right time will open up for you, so you can explain to Marc." Her father reached over and touched her, and Carrie scooted to put her arms around him.

"You are a super dad," she whispered. "And Winger is, too. I'm a lucky girl."

He patted her.

Those frightening shadows, those forboding moods of doubt that had loomed so great during the past weeks were but shadows gone, as when the sun reaches its zenith. What a relief!

In not too long, the jeep burst out of the pines and into the clearing. Winger jumped out, announcing loudly. "There are tracks all right, made after the rain. And not only jeeps have been here but motorcycles as well. Let's hope they play their games once more tomorrow!"

ELEVEN

SUPPER was eaten in silence. Weariness and hunger replaced conversation; besides, the thought of what tomorrow might bring put everyone in a somber mood. Carrie had set the food on the table and each helped himself, then went to a spot to eat quietly, thoughtfully. Carrie sat on the log next to the fire, her father nearby. She ate heartily; she was hungry! Hot or cold, Cleo's fried chicken was one thing: delicious!

Marc sat on a stump near the horses, wolfing down his food like the rest. To just sit without moving was like a sigh of relief. The horses snorted softly and blew air through their lips with a quiet whirring sound. Contented sounds. And if they were in an open field they would no doubt express complete relaxation by rolling on their backs. But that would have to wait.

The paper plates had only to be burned and the forks rinsed in the stream. An ideal way of housekeeping, Carrie thought. Winger repacked the food and secured it so the little nocturnal prowlers could not rob and nibble as the campers slept.

A forest evening does not linger on the prairie

but is lost quickly in the closeness of the towering pines. Mr. Courtley and Winger took to their sleeping bags once the dark was upon them. The trip was not one of pleasure and it was best to sleep. Who would know what the morning would bring? With that worry, sitting beside a campfire was a hollow peace.

After checking the horses, Marc, too, intended to take to his sleeping bag, but as he walked across the small clearing there was Carrie, sitting alone by the fire. She sat with her chin on her knees, her arms wrapped about her legs and her soft, thick hair fell like a shawl around her shoulders. She stared into the flickering fire seemingly unaware that Marc stood close by, looking down at her.

"Are you going to sleep soon?" he asked simply. She looked so small and lonely.

She shook her head. "No, I'm not really sleepy yet."

Carrie was wound up, and although the day had been long, if she went to bed now, she knew she would just lie there staring into the dark. The fire was better.

"Want me to sit with you for a while?" he asked, not wanting to leave her alone.

Her response was casual. "If you want to." The offhand tone didn't reflect her true feelings. She was so nervous she could barely sit still.

He sat down beside her on the log. Close by was a small pile of firewood, and Marc took a couple of pieces and put them on the fire. It sizzled and crackled as the greedy flames leaped to devour the fresh firewood. By now, the night noises had started up in the forest, so along with the snap of the fire came a chorus of peeps, chirps, and croaks. Then the stream added its endless rippling song as if to blend it all together.

The silence between them was not totally uncomfortable. The intensity of the forest itself was a humbling experience and to sit in the midst of its immensity was peaceful. No talking could match that comfort.

But Carrie did finally speak. "When will you go to the university?" she asked Marc.

It was a sudden question, completely apart from the present reality and Marc started as if jerked from a deep reverie. His answer was brisk. "I go about the first of September."

Carrie followed up with, "My brother would have attended the university . . . so will I." Then with only a slight pause, she added, "My mother told you about Allen, didn't she?"

He nodded, then shifted his feet. He cleared his throat nervously.

"You would have liked Allen. Everyone did," Carrie said, smiling into the fire. Marc was sitting very close and she would have to turn to see his face.

Marc's feet shifted again; his fingers interwove, then loosened, but he didn't answer.

"And," Carrie continued, "he would have liked you."

Marc put his hands on his knees and began to drum his fingers. He cast a sideward glance at Carrie, but she was still gazing into the fire. He spoke firmly, "You don't have to talk about your brother to me." The words were sharply directed, making the wall that still existed between them very apparent. As far as Marc was concerned, he was clearly summer help who would go away in September. She had made that clear by her question of his leaving. And now, he was a convenient listening post, although he wasn't sure why. It did not fit the pattern of her former behavior.

Carrie's heart began to flutter. She was flustered and she knew this wasn't going right. It was awkward, stiff. Marc didn't know what she was trying to do. How could she tell him that she was sorry for the way she had treated him. She had to at least do that. She certainly couldn't tell him that she liked him. The thought gave her goose bumps. She was scared, but she had started.

"Marc, I want to talk about him," she replied meekly. "Do you mind listening?"

Not sure about any of this, his answer was brief. "No, go ahead."

Carrie swallowed. Her throat was dry and choked. His voice was so sharp and cold. Tears threatened. Maybe they should just say good night, and leave things as they were by avoiding one another. Her courage almost left, but Marc made no move to leave even when she failed to speak. Well, she suddenly decided, she'd tell him straight out. That's it! Straight out. She didn't know any other way.

The tightness in her throat pulled like a noose. Could she even speak? What if he didn't believe her? Then everything would be worse.

When she finally managed to speak, her voice was funny and small, "Marc, what I want to say is that I am sorry for the way I've treated you." There, it was said.

"It's all right, I understand," he answered. His voice was not particularly friendly. He put another piece of wood on the fire. Not that it needed one, but he needed to do something.

"No, it isn't all right," she came back. Her courage began to flow again. His aloof attitude needled the fight in her. "Did you know that I disliked you the first day that you came to the ranch? It was because you stared at me. I thought you were arrogant. I actually hated you because you rode a horse so well and that you had a mustang. Did you know that?"

She spoke intensely, and Marc was taken back by her open honesty. No one had even said things like that to him before. Coming from Carrie, and knowing how he really felt about her, it hurt. What he had suspected all along was true. She did hate him.

Carrie went right on. "I disliked you riding my brother's horse and my father calling you son, when you weren't. I disliked you most because you made me think of my brother. That, and that I always acted horrid toward you. But you were always kind to me. Did you know that?"

"Not at first," came his answer, cool and impersonal, trying to mask the deep hurt.

"But when you saw that I could not ride well because I wasn't moving as one with Morning Star, you really made me mad. But my parents had been jarred loose just by his appearance on the ranch, and that her struggle and pain had took your side. They said you were right, and they made me see what was wrong. And then, I was more determined than ever to shut you out," Carrie said strongly. It was as if something had finally come loose inside, as if a floodgate had opened and everything flowed out, words and feelings, in one big gush.

"Why are you telling me all this now?" Marc asked harshly.

Carrie sat staring into the fire, silent. Why did fires make one stare, hypnotized by the dancing flames? She sighed. Her father and Winger were already asleep. Their deep steady snores joined the chorus of night noises.

Quietly Carrie said, "Because I am truly sorry, Marc. It was like I was hating you because you were alive and my brother was dead, and I didn't, and couldn't understand my feelings. Somehow riding out here, away from everything, it became clear what I was doing. I disliked you for something that was wrong with me."

The mountain air cooled gradually but steadily. The fire felt better than an hour ago. A piece of half-burned wood broke, sizzling and crackling.

"And tomorrow, I may see the horse that killed Allen. I hated that black mare, too," she said in a hoarse whipser.

Marc shifted on the log so he could look at Carrie. He gazed at her for a while in amazement. He fully realized the extreme anguish that been genuine, as was her open outpouring now. He was glad that he had held his line quietly and firmly. Yes, he had no regrets about that. On the other hand he marveled at Carrie's ability to admit that she had been victimized in her own tangled web of grief. Maybe his firmness had helped her see that. He didn't know.

"Why did you come back here if you might see the horse?" Marc wanted to know, his interest now aroused.

"I had to Marc. I have to see that horse again. Does that make any sense?" she asked.

He said thoughtfully, "Yes, I think so, Carrie."

The wood was fast becoming embers and the night was growing colder, reminding them they wore only sweaters.

"We had better get some sleep," Marc suggested. "And it is cold."

"Yes. I'm sleepy now. It has been a long day," Carrie agreed.

They stood up, almost as if on a signal. When they did so, their shoulders touched. Marc half-turned toward Carrie and looked directly into her face. This time Carrie sought his eyes. Facing each other, Carrie tipped her head back and searched his eyes. They remained standing, staring, for what seemed a long time. Neither spoke. There was no need. The message came through their eyes. First, a questioning glint, probing each others feelings; then wonderment, which turned to a deep feeling of . . . what? Neither was sure.

Marc's own attitude began to crumble. Was

it possible? Did Carrie feel for him, in the way he really felt for her? Could he trust what he seemed to read in her eyes? He controlled an intense urge to gather her to him, and instead said, "I'll take care of the fire."

Carrie nodded, her eyes still locked with his. She could scarcely breathe. *Do I have a chance,* she thought. *Is that what he is saying . . . that he likes me?* It seemed to be there in his eyes. "Good night, Marc," she whispered.

"Good night, Carrie," he answered in a voice barely audible, for he could scarcely trust himself to speak.

Settled in her sleeping bag under the slanting protection of the pup tent, Carrie sighed. A happy, contented sigh. From her innermost being that glowing warmth of forgiving love spread through her. She heard Marc outside banking the fire and checking the campsite to the snoring accompaniment of her dad and Winger. It was all a comfort, peaceful. The summer was not over, and perhaps the final touch would be far more gentle than the stark awakening of the first months. She was sure of it. Drowsiness became the pathway to sleep, and Carrie slept soundly.

Shouting awoke her abruptly. It was barely daylight. Dressing quickly, she crawled out of the tent to see what Winger was shouting about so loudly. Something was happening in the valley, that was for sure. By the time she reached the opening in the trees so that she could see down into the valley, Winger and her dad were heading down the hillside in the jeep. Marc came to stand beside her to watch.

"The horses!" Carrie exclaimed in awe.

There they were! It was hard to believe she was actually seeing them. What a beautiful sight! One that her brother had viewed time after time, until he had decided which horse he must have for his own. The fatal decision.

Marc stood calmly behind Carrie. Although the scene below intrigued him also, he was more aware of Carrie, of her long hair that touched him, and just her nearness.

It was difficult to say how many horses there were, but they stayed fairly close, like any herd of animals, but there was also a wariness. There was every color, and they looked like a marbleized centerpiece gracing the spreading green of the lush mountain meadow. The lead stallion stood apart, nervous, and with good reason, for out of the hills came a high whining sound.

Then the enchantment turned to distress, as from one side of the valley two motorcycles shot out at full speed, and closed in on the grazing band.

"Winger was right!" Carrie gasped. I don't believe it!"

Marc, too, became alert to the happenings below them.

As the men approached the horses, the frightened creatures began to scatter and run. When the horses separated, each trying to escape the oncoming threat, Carrie saw the black mare. Involuntarily, she reached back and grabbed Marc's arm and whispered, "There she is! The black mare! Do you see her?"

"Yes, Carrie, I do," Marc answered gently. "She's a magnificent animal." He shifted Carrie's hand and put it in his own, and she eagerly grasped his hand in return. They stood hand-in-hand, watching the scenerio in the valley. Oh, Carrie was so glad Marc was here.

With the horses scattered, the men had to decide which to chase for their fun and games. It was the black mare that they chose. She ran like lightning, streaking across the meadow. But she seemed to be searching for something, for she circled back toward four other horses. Then from their protective shelter came a colt, and it ran straight to the black mare.

"A colt! She has a colt!" Carrie shouted, grasping Marc's hand even tighter. And in horror, they watched as the two men headed their motor-cycles directly at them.

"No! No!" Carrie screamed. "Not Allen's horse!"

Suddenly, she jerked her hand away. "Oh, Marc, I nearly forgot!" She ran to the pup tent, and when she returned she had a camera with a telephoto lens. "Dad told me to take pictures if anything happened in the valley."

She was nervous, but one by one she snapped pictures of the men on the motorcycles. After a number of shots, she stopped to wipe away some tears. "Where are Dad and Winger?" she cried. As she spoke, the jeep roared off the hillside into the opening.

"I wonder if your dad can ever catch those two with a jeep?" Marc questioned with concern.

And he was right, for the men shot across the valley at high speeds. They sped close to the mare and her colt, then turned sharply to come back at them again. The mare didn't know how to confront or come to terms with the motor- cycles, which were so far removed from any of nature's threats. She continued to stand between her offspring and the oncoming attack.

The men were so engrossed in the chasing that they were not aware of the jeep, nor did they appear to be concerned about any interference. Obviously, they thought themselves completely isolated form the outside world or from anybody. The rest of the horses had by this time begun to enter the safety of the hills, but the lead stallion kept running back into the valley, not wanting any of his horses to come to harm.

Then one of the motorcycles decided to in- clude the stallion in his chase, for he swung the cycle sharply in his direction, but in the tight turn the cycle whirled out of control, spinning itself high into the air. The driver flew in the opposite direction.

"Oh!" both Carrie and Marc exclaimed, se- cretly glad that something had stopped him. Carrie took a few more pictures, then put the camera down on the ground. She glanced up at Marc, who had his eyes fixed on the assault in the valley.

"Now maybe they'll stop!" Carrie declared vehemently.

"Let's hope so," Marc replied. "And I think they will."

He was right. The other man twisted his head to see where his friend had gone and, on seeing his plight, quickly spun his machine about and raced toward him. At the same time, however, he became aware of the jeep heading across the valley toward them both. This added confusion, for he now had to make a choice between his own escape and his stranded friend. He chose escape and whizzed over the meadow to vanish among the trees. The whine of the cycle could be heard trailing off into the hills.

By the time Winger and Mr. Courtley reached the downed man, he was standing, apparently unharmed, for he walked to his motorcycle. The three men began to talk in earnest, and finally they all climbed into the jeep, leaving the motorcycle lying in the grass.

In the meantime, the mare realized she was free from the frightening cycles and guided her colt back toward the hills. She slowed her pace to accommodate her baby, and the stallion galloped to join them. The three ran with determined grace to the waiting band that was already among the sheltering trees.

"Run!" Carrie hollered. "Run!" Then she took one last picture of the three horses. "She is beautiful, isn't she, Marc? I see now why Allen wanted her so."

"She is a beauty! That is the kind of horse my ancestors would have chosen for their stock when they depended on the wild horse to build their bands," Marc said. There had been a thrill in seeing the mustangs in their wild setting.

"Go! go!" Carrie quietly urged, until the three disappeared into the wooded slopes. Then in a hushed voice, she said, "I don't hate her anymore. I don't. I just hope those men never come back in here again. That mare belongs to Allen and always will."

As Carrie stood gazing after the horses, as if she could still see them, the tears began to flow. Tears of relief. Tears that released the pent-up anxieties. Suddenly she felt as free as the mare.

"No, you don't hate, Carrie. Anyone who loves horses as much as you do could not hate a magnificent animal like that. Allen loved her. Respect that, for him." Marc spoke carefully, softly.

"There was a time I would have gladly killed that horse . . . I did it over and over in my mind," Carrie confided through the tears. "Isn't that terrible?" She closed her eyes as if to shut out even the memory. "But now I will remember her as we saw her today . . . skimming across the meadow like a bird in flight. And a colt, too. That was special."

"Everything is all right, Carrie," Marc said softly. "And, you're all right, too. Do you know that?"

She turned to face him. "Yes," she murmured. Looking up at him, she thought him the most wonderful person in the world.

The sun, just beginning its ascent above the rim of the hills on the far side of the valley, touched the gold in Carrie's chestnut hair, setting it aflame. Marc smiled at her, his hazel eyes warm and accepting. He reached and pulled her close to him. Carrie buried her face in the softness of his shirt and cried while Marc encircled her tightly in his arms.

The wall that had existed over the past weeks, crumbled further, and Marc could scarcely believe that the feelings he had for Carrie could be expressed. And Carrie, wrapping her arms around Marc, felt secure, though the tears flowed like an ever-bubbling mountain spring; and in the secret places of her heart she was glad Debbie had been right.

After a while the tears became intermittent, hushed sobs. Shortly, Carrie lifted her head to look up at Marc again. Her eyes were red and fringed with wet eyelashes, but to Marc, she was beautiful, tear-streaked face, and all. Holding each other, their feelings spilled out through their eyes, and Carrie didn't mind one bit that Marc stared at her; and Marc, now sure there was not one brick left of that cold wall, bent to kiss her tenderly, firmly, and it was not the kiss of a brother.